Father to the Man

Father to the Man
and other stories

Adrian Plass

HarperCollins*Publishers*

HarperCollins*Publishers*
77–85 Fulham Palace Road, London W6 8JB

First published in Great Britain
in 1997 by HarperCollins*Publishers*

1 3 5 7 9 10 8 6 4 2

Adrian Plass asserts the moral right
to be identified as the author of this work

Copyright © 1997 Adrian Plass

A catalogue record for this book is
available from the British Library

ISBN 0 551 030828

Printed and bound in Great Britain by
Caledonian International Book Manufacturing Ltd, Glasgow

This book is dedicated to the memory of my mother, who died before it was completed, and to her grandchildren, Stephen, Luke, Jason, William, Maya, Matt, Joe, David, Katy and 'Pod'. We shall all miss her very much.

Contents

Preface

This book is about fathers and sons, death, heaven, marriage, the way in which the past can, for better as well as worse, reach a long arm into the present, and, naturally, just a little about cricket. In other words, it is, as all my books have been, exactly where I happen to be in my life and in my thinking at the present time.

I seem to remember C.S. Lewis remarking in one of his essays that almost every assumption ever made about him by a critic on the basis of what he had written was completely inaccurate. In this context it may be interesting to note that the story called 'Posthumous Cake', which concerns the way in which a family reacts to the death of Granny Partington, their oldest member, was actually written long before the others. My own mother, a very important part of my life, died while I was in the middle of writing this book, and it would be perfectly reasonable for some future biographer (assuming that anyone was mad enough to want to write about my life) to assume that 'Posthumous Cake' is directly connected with that very sad event. In fact, it is the story entitled 'Nothing but the Truth' which most closely approaches an anatomy of the pain and confusion that I experienced, and am still experiencing, in the weeks after her death. And, of course, those feelings have, consciously or unconsciously, fed into most of the writing that you will find in this book (including humorous bits – my mother would be aghast if she thought that her passing had signalled the commencement of a morbid phase in my work). There is no doubt that the stark reality of losing, not just someone whom I loved, but also someone who unconditionally loved me, has wonderfully sharpened my focus on issues with which I have claimed to be deeply concerned in the past.

Am I *really* going to heaven?

Will I *definitely* be reunited with the people I have loved?

Where does the reality of Jesus touch or merge with the reality of ordinary, granular day-to-day living?

How much do we value relationships, and how should we use and protect them properly?

How can an appropriate and creative passion be released into the tedium of what passes for 'Christian living' in the case of so many of us?

Will Lawrence finally go out to bat for Hinchley, and will he avoid having to do umpire duty after he's bowled out?

These are certainly some of the important questions that I have either skated round carefully or fallen through disastrously in this book, but, as always, I have only written about things, people and situations that happen to amuse, interest or intrigue me. If these stories have a message or a question or an answer for anyone else, then that is absolutely fine, but, despite that list of heavy issues, they are stories to be enjoyed, not tracts to be exegesized, if there is such a word. People sometimes ask me why I do not write more explicit 'outreach' material. This may be a good place to point out that just about all my attempts to be openly evangelistic have been pretty useless, whereas those of my books that are either funny or speculative and questioning have been much more effective in enabling people to see their way forward in the direction of Jesus. A lot of evangelism simply doesn't work, because it is not really done for those whom God loves, but merely to scratch an evangelical itch. Here is a silly sketch I wrote for a local church when they wanted to show how it shouldn't be done as well as how it should. Do use it in your own church if you want to, but make sure it doesn't get put on by someone who has failed to realize it's a spoof!

The Outreach Dinner

M.H. = Male Host
F.H. = Female Host
M.G. = Male Guest
F.G. = Female Guest

Scene: A dinner table with two couples about to start eating.

M.H.: Shall I just say grace?
M.G.: Grace?
M.H.: Yes, we usually say just a little err...little grace.
M.G.: Oh, well, if that's what you usually do, fine, yes, carry on.
M.H.: Okay! Right, well, Lord, we just want to thank you for George and Daphne, and we ask that they should come to know the joy and the peace of your life-giving Spirit, that they will indeed invite you into their lives, and that the redemptive power of the cross of Calvary will touch their hearts RIGHT NOW! In the holy and precious name of Jesus. Hallelujah! Praise the Lord! Amen!

(*M.G. and F.G. pick up their knives and forks, but put them down again as F.H. starts to speak, still with eyes closed.*)

F.H.: I've just been given a picture by God. I'm being shown balls of fire bouncing from head to head as we sit here, and clouds of magnolia leaves drifting gently down to cover the whole table. I think something unusual is happening here tonight. (*Opens her eyes and addresses M.G.*) Don't you agree?
M.G.: (*Nodding warily*) Oh, yes, I go along with that.
F.H.: (*Brightly*) Well, let's tuck in to the Lord's provision, shall we?
F.G.: Err, would you mind passing the salt, please?
F.H.: (*Passing it*) Oh, yes, we should all be salt, shouldn't we?

M.G.: I'm sorry?

F.H.: I was just saying that we should all be salt.

F.G.: (*Puzzled*) We should all be salt?

F.H.: And light, yes. We should all be salt and light in the world until he comes.

F.G.: Until who comes?

M.G.: You're expecting another guest?

F.H.: (*In deeply significant tones as she exchanges a knowing glance with M.H.*) Yes, in a very special sense that's so true, isn't it, Tom?

M.H.: George, could I ask you a personal question?

M.G.: (*Warily*) Y-e-e-es.

M.H.: (*Into bad counsellor mode*) George, what is there *really* in your life?

M.G.: Really?

M.H.: (*Much meaningful nodding*) Yeah.

M.G.: Well, let me see now…Okay. I've been married for ten amazingly happy years to Daphne – she was my first girlfriend and I was her first boyfriend, and we've got two adorable children who are very settled at school and have some lovely friends. We've got a beautiful five-bedroom house that was left to us by an aunt, and two almost new cars so that Daphne can get around easily while I'm at work. What else? Oh, I've just been promoted, which is great because it means that I can do quite a lot of work from home, and see a lot of Daphne and the kids – they're more important than work, in any case. What else? Well, we like walking and music, and we love going to the theatre once a month. Each Friday we help with a soup-run into the East End. We're going to spend a week doing that with the kids in the holidays before going off to a little cottage we've been lucky enough to buy in Cornwall – we lend that to friends and people who couldn't afford proper holidays otherwise. Daphne's started up a local scheme for befriending lonely elderly people – we all get involved with that, and err…Oh, yes! In two years' time I'm going to take a sabbatical and we'll rent out the house, fly to North Africa, and spend six months building a hospital in one of those really poor countries. It's all arranged with my employers. Daphne and I are studying once a week to learn the local dialect. The job'll be waiting for me when I come back, and the kids won't miss out on schooling because Daphne's a trained junior teacher. (*Pause*) I think that's about it. Oh, one other thing – fancy me forgetting that! We won the lottery last week. Only about ten thousand, but we can do an awful lot of good with that, and redecorate the house, so – we're quite pleased really. Why do you ask?

(*Pause*)

M.H.: Err, nothing.
F.H.: (*She'll sort them*) George and Daphne, the point is – where do you think you're going to go after you die?
M.G.: (*Without hesitation*) East Grinstead. That's right, isn't it, Daphne?
F.G.: (*Smiling and nodding*) East Grinstead, yes, that's right.
F.H.: (*After an incredulous pause*) Why East Grinstead?
M.G.: Well, you see, we belong to a sect that believes all roads lead ultimately to East Grinstead, don't we, Daphne? (*She nods agreement as M.H. and F.H. sit with their mouths open*) Look, I'm sorry, we've been kidding you along a bit.
F.H.: (*Faintly*) So, what…?
F.G.: We're hoping we might go to heaven and be with Jesus – if possible.
M.H.: You – you mean you're Christians?
M.G.: Well, we thought we were, but err, I don't think we're quite as good at the language as you two are…
F.H.: Why didn't you tell us?
F.G.: You never asked.
M.H.: (*Standing and rather annoyed*) But the whole point of this dinner was to convert you!

M.G.: (*Amused*) Oh, dear, I hope you didn't go to too much trouble.

F.H.: (*Looks at the curtains at the end of the room*) Oh, no, of course not!

M.H.: (*Going to the curtains and pulling them back to reveal five or six people in studied attitudes of prayer*) All right everybody. Give it a rest. Same time time next week – we've got the people from number six hundred and sixty-six coming round. I'm pretty sure they're pagans. *They* won't let us down...

(*Blackout*)

Fancy a meal with that brother and sister? No, neither do I.

Finally, I would just like to say that the major theme of fathers and sons is one which touches and reveals areas of my personality that I have been trying to face squarely for years, as have so many of the men I speak to, both Christian and non-Christian. Reading these stories may excavate all sorts of things. That is not necessarily a good or a bad thing, but it is almost certainly an opportunity of some kind.

I do hope you enjoy what you read, particularly perhaps the little story entitled 'Speaking Up', which was written by my son, Joe, when he was seventeen years old.

Nothing but the Truth

Dying was a doddle. It really was. I'd just come out of Boots after buying a new toothbrush and some cream for my – well, for something that didn't really matter once I was dead (a complete waste of money in that sense, of course) – and I stepped into the road without so much as a glance to right or left. A darkish green, number thirty-four, double-decker bus got me. There was no pain nor discomfort, not even any awareness of nasty squelching or crunching noises, just a sort of 'POP!' in my consciousness, and suddenly, there I was – dead.

What was going through my mind when that bus hit me? Well, I can tell you the exact answer to that question, embarrassing and absurdly trivial though it is. Dogs – that's what I was thinking about. Specifically, I was having a really good ponder about those new leads that people use nowadays. You know the ones I'm on about, don't you? The ones that mean you meet the dog first on one end of its lead, and then the owner about a quarter of a mile further on holding the other end. The ones where the plastic thing in the owner's hand looks like one of those spring-loaded metal ruler things. Presumably, I was thinking, when they press a button on it the dog comes whizzing back at eighty miles an hour and goes splat! against the handle. And I was wondering why anyone would want to have their dog on a lead that's two streets long, it being more like flying a kite than walking a dog. It won't be long, I thought, before someone patents a special two-handed lead so that you can set your dog spinning round and round in the far distance by pulling harder on one side than the other. Believe it or not, my mind was filled with this ridiculous vision of the future at the precise instant when the bus struck me, and the image remained in my imagination, virtually unaffected, for thirty seconds or so after I'd passed from life to death.

I was more than a bit worried at the time. Into my mind came a vague memory that Hamlet hadn't wanted to murder his uncle while he was in the middle of a prayer because people who died when they were praying were popularly supposed to go straight to heaven. So where would a head full of dogs get me? Perhaps I'd end up with Elvis Presley's Old Shep in some canine paradise. That was my first half-witted thought after realizing that I was dead.

The second thought was about being conscious at all. I was *so* relieved! You're going to think this sounds completely mad, but I was always more frightened of oblivion than hell – this without any first-hand experience of the infernal regions, mind you. But in the previous decade or so there had been quite a bit of discussion about whether God really could allow an eternity of suffering if he was as loving as he was supposed to be. One or two eminent scholars had arrived at the conclusion that hell was actually a sort of switching off for ever. According to them, you just ceased to exist. That was your punishment. This idea scared me to death. I couldn't handle the idea that everything would stop with my last breath. All that thinking and feeling and loving and worrying and trying and succeeding and failing just snuffed out like the stub of a candle. I couldn't bear the thought of that. What was the point of anything if it all ended in nothing? But it hadn't. I was still there, feeling just the same, but presumably invisible, having retreated a step or two on to the pavement just outside Boots.

I stood and watched for a while as passers-by gathered around the end of the bus, going pale and making breathy gasping noises, and looking up and down the street the way people do when they're waiting for someone else to come and be in charge. I wanted to tell them that they didn't have to worry because I was all right, but I knew without even thinking about it that they'd never be able to hear a dead person, so I didn't try.

An ambulance drew up noisily at last, closely followed by the police and a woman who looked as if she was probably a doctor. I cannot begin to tell you how strange it is to witness the after-effects of your own sudden extinction. Inside my head, you see, I seemed to be more or less the same as when I was still alive, but I couldn't help feeling a little confused. Here I was, standing transparently in the High Street of my home town, watching what was left of my visible self being dealt with very efficiently by the two-man ambulance crew and all the others, and although, as I've already said, I was extremely happy to be existing at all, I was also conscious of a feeling of anti-climax. I'd spent a fair proportion of my life worrying myself sick about death and the hereafter. Images of Grim Reapers and lakes of fire and the Seven Horsemen of the Thingamabob, all mixed up with nightmares and bits of epic films that I'd seen over the years, seemed to have no connection at all with the sheer ordinariness of what I was experiencing now.

After a few minutes I couldn't take any more. I just had to turn and walk slowly away from the scene of my fatal accident. Having absolutely no input into such a significant event in my own history was disconcerting and rather coldly alienating. Apart from anything else, I suddenly became terribly sad thinking of how my family and friends would react when they heard what had happened to me. I wished there was some way of communicating with them, some means of passing on the fact that I was still alive in some way even though I was dead. Being hit by a double-decker bus is such crushingly bad news.

Perhaps I ought to go home and try to make contact with my wife. But how would I get there? Would I walk? I never had been able to drive. Were dead people able to use public transport like everyone else? Could I think myself there by an effort of the will? Perhaps I'd be able to float. I tried a little experiment. Closing my eyes tight shut I willed myself to leave the ground and fly, as I had done on quite a number of occasions in my dreams whilst I was still alive. Sometimes, on waking from such dreams, I had been filled with an indescribably thrilling certainty that I actually had located the specific muscle which would make flight possible. Invariably disappointed, of course, I had often expressed to my wife the hope that I would be allocated wings of some sort when I got to wherever I was going once my three score years and ten came to an end. On opening my eyes now, however, I found myself still firmly rooted to the pavement, totally ignored by all the living people around me, and feeling faintly resentful that, even after having had more than a third of my statutory allowance of years chopped off so abruptly, I was still unable to take to the air.

In fact, the whole thing began to feel increasingly annoying and odd. Although it was clear that I couldn't be seen, I wasn't able to walk through solid walls, which might have been quite fun. I tried it, making, in the process, the uncomfortable and rather unexpected discovery that it was still possible to experience pain. Nor did passers-by walk through me, or I through them as in all the best ghost stories. There seemed to be a natural path-clearing process designed to ensure that I could never make physical contact with any of these distracted folk, busily going about their warm and visible lives. I decided I wouldn't bother trying to get home. The idea of being there, seeing people I loved, and not being able to get through to them, was just too dismally awful for words.

Disconsolately, I strolled to the end of the High Street and, following the road where most of the restaurants were located, headed in the direction of the seafront. Crossing the main road by the fish-and-chip shop (would I be needing food now that I was dead?) I took two flights of steps to the lower promenade and stomped along in the wind for a while with my hands buried deep in my pockets. Eventually I came to a place where the pathway narrowed a little as it curved behind an old Victorian bandstand. The wind was very high and gusty today, sweeping the tide in as far as it would go, and crashing it with tireless, rhythmic insistence against the massively thick wall that supported the promenade. I stopped and leaned over the safety railing, closing my eyes and recalling suddenly, as the flying spray soaked my dead face and hair, all those times when my wife and I had driven the eight or nine miles from where we lived down to the coast on days like this, simply because the weather was wonderfully wild. Our favourite thing of all had been watching the great clouds of white spray thrown up by the waves as they made thunderous contact with the blocks of stone beneath our feet. Those huge lumps of granite had dumbly and successfully resisted such attacks for more than a hundred years.

I started to feel very miserable indeed. Being dead hadn't been much fun so far. Nor, come to think of it, had it been very spiritual or theological, as far as I could see. Where were the angels? Where was the Eternal City whose streets were supposed to be paved with gold? Where was my heavenly mansion, specially prepared for me by – you know? If it came to that, where was *he*, for goodness' sake? At the very least, where was the long dark tunnel with a light shining in the distance and the conversation at the far end with an impressively authoritative person in which I got to be offered a choice about whether I wanted to come back or not? I remembered hearing about lots of people who hadn't actually died, or had died then been revived, who had reported something along those lines. Where was *my* tunnel, and where were the other countless billions of other dead people, and what was going to happen to me? I was on my own and unhappy and wet and dead.

So deeply did I begin to sink into this sludge of self-pity, that it was some moments before, with my eyes still closed, I registered the fact that something had changed. All the sounds and sensations of wind, sea and spray had completely ceased, and out of the silence came a woman's voice.

'Mister Porter, my name is Miss Jordan. Would you be kind enough to follow me?'

I nearly overbalanced and fell into the sea with the shock, but it wouldn't have mattered, because when I did stand up and open my eyes, the sea and the railing and the weather had disappeared, together with every other trace of my original surroundings. Instead, I found myself standing in a very plain, grey-painted corridor (not exactly a tunnel, but close enough, I reckoned), confronted by a brisk-looking, cardiganed lady in her mid-thirties, with kind eyes, who was obviously waiting for a reply. She didn't look any more dead than I felt. I decided to check one or two things before following her anywhere, no matter how kind her eyes might be. I made a feeble attempt to tidy my hair, wondering vaguely as I did so why it wasn't wet any more.

'Err, could I ask you a question? Would that be all right?'

'Two questions if you wish,' she replied, all firmness and niceness. I stared at her.

'Two?'

'Two.'

'Right – well, here's the first one.' I took a deep breath. 'Am I dead?'

'That's a nice easy one,' she said, smiling. 'Yes, Mister Porter, I am able to state quite unequivocally that you *are* dead. A large bus terminated your earthly existence just outside Boots the Chemist less than an hour ago. Do you remember the Parrot Sketch?'

'Yes, of course, it was one of the Monty...'

'Well, you are an ex-person, and indeed, all the other things that the famous parrot was, Mister Porter. And your second question?'

I wasn't sure how to put it. 'Well, you know. Am I...? Will I be...?'

'You'd like to know what will happen in the next stage of your existence?'

'Err, yes, I would.'

'Are you worried, Mister Porter?'

A funny thing happened at that moment. I never had been very good at admitting weakness, especially to women for some reason. Anything like tender loving care coming in my direction made me shrink inside and panic as if I was afraid the carer was trying to steal power from me. I opened my mouth to say that I wasn't really worried, just a little bit apprehensive, and that she surely must see how perfectly understandable that was, given the circumstances, but the words just didn't – or wouldn't – come out. Instead, I heard, with profound consternation, my own voice telling something that sounded horribly like the truth.

'Yes! Yes, actually, I feel very, very confused and frightened. I was alive a few minutes ago, and then I wasn't, and then I walked up to the bandstand, and then I was suddenly not at the bandstand because I was here, and I was wet, and I was suddenly dry, and – and now I don't know what's going to happen and I don't know who you are and, yes, I *am* worried, and I *do* want to know what's going to happen next.' Something important occurred to me. 'Oh, yes, and I don't know if you're the person to tell, but I've changed my mind about preferring hell to oblivion...'

This ragged, emotional speech disturbed me a great deal, but it made little or no impact on the efficient-looking Miss Jordan, other than to cause a slight raising of her eyebrows.

'You are in the outer reception area of the Allocations Department, Mister Porter. If you would care to follow me, I shall take you along to the Waiting Room and you will be seen very soon by a member of our assessment team.' She started to turn away, then stopped and cocked her head on one side. 'As far as hell is concerned, I seem to recall that the Anglican Church – you were a regular attender at an Anglican Church, were you not, Mister Porter?'

'Mmm, that's right,' I mumbled, adding hastily and rather pathetically, 'it was a *renewed* Anglican church.'

'I seem to recall,' she went on, 'that the Anglican Church more or less abolished hell in the mid-nineties, so perhaps we should assume that heaven and oblivion are the only remaining options?'

I looked at her in silence for a moment. For all I knew this could be God in disguise (or, as anything seemed possible now that I was dead, God *not* in disguise!) testing my sense of humour or something. I decided I'd better find out.

'Was that a joke?'

'Yes,' she said, 'it was a joke – we do have them here – but your decision to plump for oblivion after all is a very wise one, if I may say so.'

Panic!

'You don't mean that I...?'

But she had turned abruptly and was setting off at such a pace that I only just managed to catch her up as she reached a place where the passage turned sharply to the left. After that our progress to the Waiting Room (whatever that might turn out to mean) seemed to take for ever and ever. The journey was an eternity of grey-painted corridor, dimly lit by an invisible light source and unrelieved by pictures, windows or decorations of any kind, involving maze-like turnings to the left and right, interspersed with long, straight sections. All there was in the world – or in this world where I found myself now that I was definitely dead – was Miss Jordan's bobbing back, the rhythmic clacking of her heels on the lino-covered floor, and the dream-like, grey sameness of my surroundings.

Perhaps this *is* hell, I thought. Perhaps, for me, it has turned out to be a woman's back, an uncomfortably hurried walk that will never end, and acres of unrelieved, grey gloom. If so, it wasn't *too* bad. Well – not as bad as it might have been, anyway. Perhaps some delicate little refinements were to be introduced as time went by. Supposing I found that I desperately needed to go to the toilet? Maybe that would be it. There didn't appear to be doors of any kind in the walls, let alone ones that were surmounted by little stick-figures indicating facilities for GENTS or LADIES. What a hell that would be, to find yourself in a perpetual state of urgently needing to empty your bladder, but never being able to find anywhere to do it.

It made me feel better, thinking silly things like that as I stumbled along behind my guide. And they were silly thoughts, of course. After all, if there were to be no marriages in heaven, toilets were bound to be unisex, if they were needed at all. I knew what I was really doing. I was trying to distract myself from worrying about that awful phrase that Miss Jordan had used in such an emotionless way just now. She had said that I was in the 'Allocations Department'. Obviously, it was me that was going to have some destination or fate allocated to me, presumably by a member of the equally terrifyingly-entitled 'Assessment Team', somebody who, even now, was crouched slaveringly at the other end of the corridor, waiting to assess me before savagely consigning my soul to one choice torment or another.

Miss Jordan seemed to be increasing her pace, and I had to raise my own performance a gear or two to keep up with her. As I did so, there flashed quite abruptly into my mind, memories of the nineteen-sixties, when, as young Christians, my friends and I had been introduced to a series of little postcard-sized comic-books. Produced in America, they depicted in dark, petrifyingly vivid images the fate that would undoubtedly befall those who were foolish enough to die having failed to 'get their hearts right with God'.

I recalled a particularly unpleasant example, in which one such foolish fellow (I don't think any women were condemned in these publications) arrived at the place of judgement to discover that he was obliged to sit before a large screen in order to witness a film record, not just of his sins, but also of the moment when an opportunity to repent and turn to Jesus had actually been offered to him. Full of anguish now that it was too late, he watched himself contemptuously rejecting this offer, airily expressing a preference for being immersed in worldly, sinful things, and thereby missing out on the chance for his soul to be saved. In the final, nightmarish scenes, this wretched individual, still rather plaintively dressed in his expensive, worldly suit, was shown being prodded by grinning devils with pitchforks towards a lake of fire, screaming out and begging in vain as he fell, for 'one more chance' to put things right.

The last picture of all in this warmly encouraging little tract was a whole double-page spread given over to a panoramic view of hell, showing countless numbers of similarly tormented souls bobbing about in a sort of vast barbecue, crying out in agony of body and spirit, knowing that they were forever damned to endure, without relief, the pain of being burned alive.

These 'evangelistic tools', as I remembered them being described, were supposed to be left lying around by us keen members of the youth group, in places where unsaved young people might happen upon them by chance, and thus be terrified into understanding the love of God. I suppose they were a form of spiritual anti-holiday brochure. In later years I had laughed heartily with Christian friends about those little books. We had wondered how we could possibly have taken such dangerous rubbish seriously. Now, as I pursued the ever-accelerating figure in front of me in the direction of my 'assessment', and mentally surveyed a succession of those hideously gothic images, I was unable to raise the faintest glimmer of a smile. I felt sick with fear. Miss Jordan was right. Oblivion suddenly looked very sweet.

But what of free will? As the ever-increasing speed of our journey forced me to break into a slow, awkward trot, I found myself wondering if the right to make decisions about my own movements had been taken away when that bus finished me off earlier. After all, a lot of other things seemed to be working in the way that they had always done. I was thinking and feeling and seeing and hearing, just as I had when I was alive. And Miss Jordan had *asked* me to follow her just now. There had been no sense of being forced to go anywhere or do anything. I asked myself what would happen if I simply stopped. Why shouldn't I stop? Would I be told off if I did? Would Miss Jordan tell me off? Would she fail to notice that I was no longer behind her and wonder where I'd got to when she arrived at the mysterious 'Waiting Room'?

The pace had gradually continued to increase, to such an extent that I was now literally running to keep up. Miss Jordan, on the other hand, seemed to be moving with a smooth gliding motion, as though she was on castors or rails instead of two human feet. Panic took away what little breath I had left as my mind filled with the ludicrous notion that I might have become a helpless Mario-like character in someone else's giant video game. Sweat began to drip from my forehead into my eyes, blurring all but the outline of that fast-moving shape in front of me. I decided that I would stop. Why shouldn't I stop? I was going to stop.

I stopped.

Relief! Sinking down on to the floor, I sat back on my heels, allowed my head to hang down on my chest, and closed my eyes. All that mattered for a moment or two was the urgent need to fill my lungs with oxygen. Eventually, as my breathing returned to normal, I became uneasily aware that something had changed in the very air around me. The sweat had become clammy on my face and body, and my arms and legs had begun to shiver with cold. Opening my eyes I found that I was in freezing, noiseless, total darkness. Raising myself on to one knee, I stretched my arms out to locate the walls of the corridor, but there were no walls. I stood up and began to move tentatively, exploring more of the space around me, but still my questing fingertips met no resistance from anything at all. There was nothing but the cold and the utter darkness.

That absolute absence of light was like nothing I had ever known during my life on earth, and yet, oddly enough, it immediately triggered clear memories of a childhood experience that had not surfaced for years.

As a small boy, waking in the early hours of the morning, I had sometimes been driven by fear or loneliness to make my way along the landing to my parents' room, always the place of ultimate security for me, as I suppose it is for most small children. Once or twice, though, it had been so pitch-black on the landing outside my bedroom that I had become paralysed with fear at about the mid-point in my journey. I would remain rooted to this spot half-way along the landing for quite a long time, unable to go forward or back for fear of the night creatures that would certainly attack me as soon as they detected the slightest movement. Three or four fairly short steps in front of me, as I knew perfectly well, was the door to my parents' room. If I could just get to that door and open it everything would be fine. A streetlamp burned all night on the pavement outside their window, so that, even when the curtains were drawn, there was always enough soft yellow light to send the hungry darkness hunting elsewhere. Three short steps to safety, and yet sometimes they were far too difficult, and three too many.

Now, in this even deeper blackness, an additional memory struck me, one I had never been aware of before. Somewhere, hidden right in the centre of that awful, rigid, darkness-ridden fear, a tiny seed of cosy excitement had been at least a tiny part of the reason for not hurrying to where the light was. Part of me, I now saw, had actually enjoyed being tucked into my black envelope of nothingness, and as I thought and wondered about that strange piece of truth I began dimly to perceive why.

It had to do with the fact that my very earliest recollections of being alive were heavy with an aching dread of vague, shadowy enemies who offered a constant, lowering threat, even though they were invisible and impossible to identify. And the greatest terror of all, played out over and over again in my imagination, was that these ever-watchful demons were going to pounce in an unguarded moment and make me die purely from the explosive shock of their attack. That was why doing ordinary, safe things was so dangerous. You forgot about the demons. You gave them chances to get you. Standing on the landing in the dark as a small child brought me as near as I would ever dare go to a place right outside the entrance to the cave where those monsters lived. They might still kill me, but they wouldn't be able to surprise me, and that was the most important thing of all. Out there on the landing – I was in charge.

I shivered again with cold and unhappiness. Why was I thinking things I'd never thought before, in a place where I'd never been before and wanted to leave behind as soon as I possibly could? Why did those distant memories suddenly seem so important? This wasn't the landing, nor was this darkness anything like the darkness of the landing. This was a place where something more than light was missing.

'I can't see the hope in front of my face.'

The whispering of my own voice frightened me, but it was the truth. I was in a place that was cold with the complete absence of possibility. I knew that if I walked or ran or staggered through this eternity of darkness for a billion years it and I would never become warmer, and my fingertips would never touch or be touched by anything or anybody at all.

'I'm dead.'

Sounds comic, doesn't it? But it is true that, for a while, the fact that I'd been recently demolished by a bus had slipped my mind. I was dead, and I was in the hopeless dark. I should have followed Miss Jordan to the Waiting Room. I shouldn't have stopped. I should have taken my chance with the assessment thingy. I should never have walked into the road so carelessly after coming out of Boots. I should have looked after my life properly. I should have paid real attention to priorities. I should never have insisted on taking charge of my own...

My miserable musings were cut short at this point by the sudden, heart-lifting realization that my right hand had accidentally made contact with something coldly metallic and oddly familiar. Reaching out to the left with my other hand I encountered the smooth surface of what felt like an emulsioned wall. At the same time the darkness began to seem less intense. A very pale light was filtering through diamond-shaped panes of glass in a window over to my right. Diamond-shaped panes of glass? It must be – it could only be...

I was back at home, in the house where I grew up. It was night-time and I was on the landing, stuck half-way between my own room and the one at the front where my parents slept. With my right hand I was clinging on to the top of the old-fashioned radiator, just as I had always done when I was little, and with my left I was trying to anchor myself to the opposite wall. It was just as it had always been, except that I wasn't little – I was big, and there were important issues at stake, if I could only work out what they were.

'Go for the light. Go on, go for it now!'

That was what I told myself to do, and that was what I obediently did. I took three steps forward, turned the handle of my parents' bedroom door, and walked in. For one strange, tearfully joy-filled moment I saw my long-dead mother and father, sitting up in bed reading contentedly, just as I had always pictured them. Turning their faces to me as I entered the room, they smiled with great warmth and no apparent surprise at all, but as I moved towards them the scene disappeared abruptly and I found myself stepping into a comfortably furnished office through a door which was being politely held open for me by Miss Jordan, looking as calm, cool and efficient as ever.

'Please take a seat, Mister Porter, one of our assessors will be with you directly. Would you care for coffee?'

Coffee? After death? Surely not.

'I'd love a coffee, thanks. Err, black with one sugar please. By the way, Miss Jordan, I'm really sorry I didn't keep up with you. Didn't you say that I had to – well, shouldn't I have gone to the Waiting Room before coming here?'

She smiled faintly. 'You have just come from the Waiting Room, Mister Porter. I'll get your coffee, shall I? Black, with one sugar, wasn't it? And a biscuit?'

'Yes. Yes, thank you.'

Biscuits as well!

I was beginning to feel like Alice in Wonderland. Curiouser and curiouser. As Miss Jordan closed the door behind her I glanced around the office. Apart from the fact that, as in the grey corridor, there were no windows, nothing distinguished it or its contents from any other office I'd ever seen during my lifetime. There was a large leather-topped desk with a rather old-fashioned-looking telephone on it and, somewhat puzzlingly in the circumstances, a free-standing clock of the old chiming variety, three comfortable, upright chairs matching the one I was sitting on, and a number of very pleasing pictures on the walls, including a couple of large, richly painted landscapes and a very fine portrait in oils of a youngish man. In the corner stood a grey filing cabinet with five drawers and, on top of it, a pot containing a plant with a knobbly stalk and big, green, shiny leaves. Despite the extraordinary succession of events since my death I was even more surprised by the filing cabinet than I had been by the clock. It seemed strange that such a very solid means of information storage should be needed or necessary in the ethereal realms. And what about computers? Were there no computers in heaven? How could the names and records of all the countless billions of people who had existed throughout history be contained in five drawers? Mind you, nothing was turning out as I would have expected anyway. What was a mere filing cabinet compared to the brief encounter with my deceased parents that I had just experienced and which was still making my head spin? I wondered if I would be allowed to see them again. Surely...

What was that on the desk?

I leaned forward. What was that lying on the desk beside the telephone? What was that flattish, cardboard thing? It was an orange-coloured file. There was a file on the desk. Craning my neck I saw that a name was printed on the front.

MARTIN JOHN PORTER

My file was lying there, not much more than an arm's length away. MY FILE, presumably a no-holds-barred account of both my public and private lives, was sitting on that desk waiting to be opened and looked at and used to decide whether I would be convicted and despatched to the barbecue, or allowed to go to the place where I was sure my parents had gone. It suddenly occurred to me that those sixties 'evangelistic tools' of ours never got round to depicting heaven, other than in illustrations of mild, modestly dressed, happy American people, queuing on rather improbably dramatic, twisting mountain pathways as they waited with admirable Christian patience for it to be their turn to pass through the Pearly Gates. Now I came to think about it, people in the various churches I'd belonged to had always been much clearer about hell than they were about heaven.

I was just toying with the idea of reaching across to helpfully square up the corner of the file with the corner of the desk, when the door opened and Miss Jordan reappeared with my coffee and biscuit on a tray. She was closely followed by a tall, pleasantly ordinary-looking man in a smart dark suit. He must have been about thirty-five, with neatly combed, wavy fair hair and a relaxed, genial, non-threatening manner. He extended an arm to shake my hand. When he spoke, the friendliness of his tone and the sincerity of the smile that accompanied his words were all most reassuring.

'Mister Porter, how nice to meet you. My name is Philip Hammond – please call me Philip. I'm a member of the assessment team, and we shall be spending about half an hour together.'

'Oh, not eternity, then,' I joked feebly and nervously.

He laughed politely, but didn't actually respond to what I'd said. Pulling out a chair and sitting down on the other side of the desk, he leaned back and continued to smile at me, drumming lightly on the edge of the desk with his fingertips as he did so. I waited. I stirred my coffee. After a while the silence drove me into speaking again.

'I was thinking just now, err, Philip – it is Philip, isn't it?'

'Philip, yes, that's right, please call me Philip.' He nodded encouragingly.

'Well, just now when I was following – when I was on my way here, I was thinking about some really silly books we used to look at when I first became a Christian. Little – err, little sort of books, they were. Postcardish sort of size. They had awful pictures in them of what hell was going to be like, all flames and devils and people screaming in a great sort of pit. Really frightening stuff. We were terrified for a bit that it was really going to be like that. We realized how silly it was later on, of course. I mean, it's just – it's just not…is it?'

I had allowed a little light laugh to lift my voice as I spoke these words, my dearest wish being that the man sitting opposite would echo my ripple of amusement. We would enjoy a jolly good chuckle together about the absurdity of ever imagining that human beings might end up in such an appalling state. But there was no such reassuring echo. He just went on smiling at me. I wanted to die. But I couldn't. I already had. He leaned forward, resting his folded arms on the desk.

'Mister Porter – may I call you Martin?'

'Yes, yes, of course. I'd rather you did.'

Surely, I thought, you don't deliberately get on to Christian name terms with a man just before arranging for him to be dropped into a fiery pit for the rest of eternity, do you? Surely…

'Martin, am I right in thinking that you're a little puzzled about' – he spread his hands out and looked from one side of the office to the other – 'all this?'

'It is a bit surprising,' I said, taking my first sip of as good a cup of coffee as I'd ever tasted. 'I suppose if I'm honest I was expecting something a tad more – well, epic, I suppose. A bit more like Revelation.'

'The book of Revelation, you mean?'

'Yes,' I warmed a little to my theme, 'you know the sort of thing I mean – vast cataclysmic scenes with horsemen, and thousands of martyrs, and trumpets, and fire falling from heaven, and giant candlesticks and err, well, scrolls being eaten,' I finished rather lamely.

'Scrolls being eaten?'

'Well, perhaps…'

'That's what you expected?'

'I didn't expect biscuits.' I took a bite. The biscuit was heaven. I spoke through a mouthful of crumbs. 'The thing that's so strange is that it's such a mixture. Being in that cold, dark place just now was really weird and scary, and then I was suddenly back in my house and I saw my parents, and that was even weirder, and now I'm sitting in this office with you eating biscuits and drinking coffee, and it's as ordinary as…as…' I searched around in my experience for the epitome of ordinariness. 'It's as ordinary as Luton.'

'Luton?'

'Luton, yes.'

'Are you glad that it's ordinary – this bit, I mean?'

'Well, I'm not sure.' I brushed biscuit crumbs from my pullover. 'It's quite sort of comforting, but it all depends what happens next. I mean, if I'm on my way to the sort of thing they had in those books I was talking about, it doesn't really make any difference how ordinary it all feels now, does it?'

Another opportunity for Philip Assessment-Person Hammond to dispel my most immediate fear. But he didn't. He sat back and smiled again.

I've never been any good at silences.

'That's my file, isn't it?' I said, pointing at the orange folder on the desk. 'Are we going to go through that together, or do you already know what's in it – or what? I suppose,' I went on, recalling an aspect of the situation that, incredibly, had hardly crossed my mind since dying, 'you have to decide whether I'm saved or not. Do you call it being saved up here?'

He shrugged good-humouredly. 'We do call it that sometimes, yes. Do you think you're saved, Martin?'

What to say? Would it be adjudged pride or humility if I assumed that I was a definite candidate for Paradise? A bold assertion that, yes, I was indeed saved would, at the very least, suggest the kind of strong faith that had always been considered so valuable in the church circles I had belonged to. Or perhaps it would be better to express a more low-key, quietly humble hope that, despite my many sins and failings, I might be redeemed, and invited to partake in eternal life. I could feel all the familiar church language coming back into my mind. Maybe that would be useful when I got going in a minute, but perhaps I should begin by throwing out a few solid, qualifying facts.

'Well, I was baptized by immersion when I was thirty-six.'

Listening to my own voice, I was all too aware that I must be coming over like an eighteen-year-old informing a prospective employer that I had a B grade in A-level Biology.

'Ah, now that's interesting,' replied Philip Hammond. He pulled the orange file towards him and opened it, flicking through the pages inside until he came to the entry he was looking for. 'Yes,' he said, running his finger down the sheet and stopping about half-way, 'that's most interesting. Tell me, Martin, *why* did you get baptized?'

Earlier on, when Miss Jordan had asked me if I was worried, I had tried to give her one answer and ended up giving her another. It had been a very bad attack of involuntary truth telling. The same thing happened now. In my mind I prepared an answer that was quite solidly orthodox – something about wanting to obey the command of Our Lord that all men should be baptized by water and by the Spirit, this being the water bit, of course. But that reply just wouldn't come out, however hard I tried. For a moment or two I sat in tongue-tied silence, quite incapable of using my mouth to frame the words that I had composed in my head.

'Well, I decided to do all the things that I might discover I'd needed to have done when it came to – well, to this sort of situation, I suppose. I thought if I had the whole set it would be a good insurance. I'd be well prepared.'

I was horrified by the words that were coming out of my mouth, but I didn't seem to have any choice. Or rather, I had a choice of saying nothing at all or telling the truth. Unfortunately, I was not at all confident that the truth was going to do me any good.

'The whole set?' Philip Hammond closed my file and, resting both elbows on the desk and his chin on his interlinked fingers, regarded me quizzically. 'What do you mean by the whole set?'

'You know – baptism, repentance, asking Jesus into your life. What else? Oh, yes – acknowledging the redemptive power of his death and resurrection, confessing your faith before men, all those things – the whole set. I've got them all. I was scared that I might get left behind or go to hell so I made a list of all the things I needed to do to get saved, and then I ticked them off one by one as I went along. I've done all those things. They should be in the file. Are they?'

'Hold on – we'll talk about your file again in a minute. Just going back to your baptism for a moment, the first one in the err, set. Tell me, did you give something called a testimony before going into the water?'

'Yes. Yes, I did do that, just a few words about why I was doing it – why I wanted to be baptized, that's all it was. Everyone at our church did that when they were dunked – baptized, I mean.'

'What did you say in that testimony?'

I cleared my throat. Sadly, I seemed to have total recall.

'Err, I believe I started by saying that I'd recently heard the Lord speaking very clearly about the fact that baptism was his will for me, and that I was simply being obedient to his command.'

'And was that true?'

Oh, dear.

'Do you have an equivalent up here to the fifth amendment?'

He sat back and laughed. 'You mean the thing about not having to say anything that might incriminate you? Well, we don't, but if we had you'd be very ill-advised to take advantage of it. Are you saying that you were not entirely honest in your testimony?'

I squirmed and wriggled, but there was no help for it. Out came the truth.

'Well, I certainly never actually heard God speaking directly to me about being baptized, but I sort of persuaded myself that I had a … a feeling that he was putting the idea into my mind. I really wanted to be able to say that I had been clearly called, so I just...well, tidied up the truth until it looked a bit more convincing. In any case, that was how you talked about that sort of thing at our church. I don't remember anyone ever getting up at their baptism and saying that they had a vague feeling that God could possibly be telling them to get baptized, and it was worth doing anyway, because it would be good spiritual insurance. You just didn't talk like that at our church.'

'All the ideas were in ready-made packets?'

I nodded. 'Yes, in a way, I suppose they were.'

'And what about the "simply being obedient to his command" bit?'

'Well, like I said, a lot of it was fear. Everyone seemed so *sure* – do you know what I mean?'

'Yes, I think so.'

'It was quite frightening when I looked inside myself to find just how *not* sure I was, if you know what I mean. I suppose I thought – well, if they've got it all sussed out it must make sense to go along with whatever they said you had to do. So I did.' I was silent for a moment. 'I did talk to God about it though, you know. It was the night before. I suddenly got all embarrassed about the idea of looking a twit in front of loads of people in my soaking wet nightgown. I remember it clearly because I was watching the end of "Question Time" on the television, one of my favourite programmes, so it must have been a Thursday evening. I felt so bad that I turned the TV off.'

Philip Hammond registered mock amazement. 'You actually turned it off!'

'Well, you're right, that was rather unusual. Anyway, I did turn it off and tried to...to be with God. Told him how nervous I was and asked him to help me get through it. And I said how much I wanted to have a real experience of him, right there in the sitting-room.'

'And did you?'

I wondered if I might have picked up some kind of throat complaint in that cold, dark place just now. I had the greatest difficulty in serving up the next portion of ungarnished truth.

'Hmm, I may well have been about to have a real experience of him, but just at that moment I noticed the clock and realized the snooker was coming on at any moment, so I turned the television back on and – well, kept one eye on that while I was waiting for my err… experience of God to happen.'

He tilted his head to one side and frowned at the desk for a moment. 'So, you were waiting for God to speak to you in roughly the same way that you might have kept half an eye open for the bus while you were watching the telly in a shop window just up the road from the bus-stop. Does that sum it up?'

'Well, yes, I'm afraid it does.'

'When you said at your baptism…' he studied the file for a moment, 'when you said that the Lord had "spoken clearly to you" the night before, you actually meant that he might have been going to, but you were so engrossed in the fact that Willie Thorne was heading for a possible clearance that you couldn't be absolutely sure.'

'Well…'

Philip Hammond suddenly threw back his head and laughed like a drain.

All very well, I thought, watching him, but where does all this leave me? When he's finished laughing his head off, is he going to put on some sort of divine black cap and shovel me off into the hands of those grinning devils with their pitchforks? If so, the merriment seemed more than a little inappropriate. He finished laughing at last and, wiping his eyes with the knuckle of one hand, spoke apologetically.

'Please forgive me, Martin, I really shouldn't have laughed like that. I suppose it's just that I never cease to be amazed and amused by the gap between the public face of what's known as Christianity, and the way things actually are for people who call themselves Christians. Seek the Lord with all your heart in the short gap between "Question Time" and the "World Snooker Championship". Marvellous!'

He shook his head as if to clear it, then bent over the file again, moving papers slowly from one side of the desk to the other. At last he picked one page up and studied it for a few moments. When he spoke again his voice was very soft.

'There was a time when you were much more sure, wasn't there, Martin? What happened?'

Oh, dear. Into the shadows.

'My father died.'

'Fairly recently?'

'Yes, a while before my baptism.'

'Your mother died when you were much younger, didn't she?'

'I was at boarding school. She got suddenly ill and died. Then Dad said I could stop being at boarding school because she was the only one who wanted me to go, and I was so pleased it was like being wrapped in cotton-wool. Mum dying was awful, but I was at home and Dad was there. Everything was soon all right.'

'But your father's death was different?'

I felt sick suddenly. 'Have I really got to go through all this?'

Philip Hammond didn't say a word. He just sat back in his chair quite calmly with his arms folded, waiting for me to get on with whatever I decided to do. I buried my face in my hands for a moment, fearful of the truth that I already knew so well. Oh, well, in for a penny…

Raising my head I said, 'I was feeling pretty sure about God and heaven and all that in the time leading up to when he died. Heaven especially. I really thought I'd got it all in perspective. Jesus would be waiting for us, and all the most beautiful things on earth – well, the essence of all those things would be there because – because the person who made them was going to be there.'

'What sort of things?'

'*All* sorts of things. One great long Mary Poppins list, only with different things in it – different things for each person, I mean.'

'Like a 147 snooker clearance, for instance?'

'Well, yes, I'd like to think that could be arranged for me – that would be wonderful.' I sighed ecstatically. 'But, no, seriously, I was really confident most of the time about, you know, going to be with Jesus and salvation and all the rest of it. It's true that every now and then I'd have a sudden attack of total disbelief and wonder why I wasn't out doing as many enjoyably evil things as I could before I shuffled off my mortal coil, but most of the time I felt good about it all, and I even used to tell other people what I believed. Some of them got quite interested – well, more than interested. We started a little group…'

'What happened when your father died?'

I took a deep breath, feeling all the pain of that day and so many of the days that had followed, as though some sort of emotional photograph had been taken at the moment of his death and had remained on view ever after to my inner eye.

'I was at the hospital – had been on and off for more than a fortnight. We'd been through the same pattern over and over again. Dad would seem to go right down and look as if he couldn't possibly come through, and then he'd suddenly pick up and be talking and chatting as though hardly anything was wrong at all. Two or three times I said goodnight to him before going home to get some sleep, thinking that I was really saying goodbye. And then, in the morning, there he'd be, sitting up in bed telling the nurses off because he hadn't been given any breakfast. It all got very wearing in the end – I don't mean that I wasn't pleased he pulled through each time – course I was. It was just that, in a way, you see, I was experiencing

25

all the pain of losing him every few days, followed by all the relief of still having him afterwards, and I was getting plain exhausted by this weird roller-coaster ride. And then, quite suddenly, he went. He just stopped breathing when he was asleep one morning and went.'

'You took it hard?'

'I took it in all sorts of ways. I was struck straightaway by the big gap between knowing someone's going to die, and knowing they have died. People say you can prepare yourself. I thought I had. But I hadn't really. It was a huge shock. A bit like being indoors and suddenly the whole house except for the floor you're sitting on flies up into the air and disappears into the far distance in a split second.'

Philip Hammond nodded gently but said nothing.

I remembered something.

'In the town near where I live there used to be a big supermarket about fifty yards back from the main road in the centre of town, with a Chinese restaurant over the top. So every time you walked along the High Street it was there…part of the scenery, even if you didn't actually really register it. Then, one night, there was a fire and the whole thing burned down. Nearly caught the other buildings but the firemen did a great job, apparently. Well, I read about it in the papers the next morning, and everyone was talking about it, of course, but, as it happened, I didn't have any reason to go into town for two or three days after that, and when I did I was so absorbed by whatever I was doing or looking for that I completely forgot about the fire. I'd walked about half-way up the High Street when I suddenly realized that something was all wrong.'

'There was a gap?'

'Yes, the very shape of that part of the world had changed, and because I'd forgotten about the fire I couldn't understand it. I felt as if I'd wandered into some kind of parallel universe or something. Then I remembered, of course, and felt stupid. Dad's death was a bit like that.

One huge piece of my personal scenery had gone, and I felt lost and disoriented. The world was the wrong shape. All those decades of personality and life and significance and – I dunno – sheer existence, just extinguished in an instant. Such a *big* thing to happen, and such a … a profound silence afterwards.

'The only thing was – I do remember that for two or three days after his death, we had the most amazing skies in our part of the country. Great big, extravagant brushstrokes of gold and grey and silver, with the sun pouring white light through the gaps as if the budget for special effects had been doubled. And I remember thinking that there must be some kind of celebration going on in heaven, and hoping that it might be because dad had arrived there. Made me feel quite good for a while, but only a while.'

'Were you sure he was in heaven?'

There are some questions that cannot produce anything as simple as a reply that is truthful or untruthful. I suppose I mean the kind of questions where you don't really know what you think yourself, and even if you do, there may be another reply just under the surface of what you are thinking and saying that is more true than the answer in the front of your mind. This question from Philip Hammond was like that, and I was interested, in view of my newly acquired truth-telling mechanism, to discover what kind of response I would offer him. I found myself looking into the past and seeing my father's dead face on the pillow as I had seen it only minutes after his death.

'The thing is…' This was difficult. 'The thing is that he was *so dead*. He was so dead.' I felt a sob rising in my throat. 'He was as dead as it's possible to be. He'd dropped out or gone away from that thing lying on the hospital bed, and it was as if a giant full-stop had gone splat! on the end of his life. Of course, all my Christian mechanism creaked into gear – he'd gone to heaven, we would meet again – all that. But…'

'But what?'

The truth.

'There was a little fear in me, a … a little dark bud of panic.'

'A fear of what?'

'A fear of nothing. A fear that there was nothing. A fear that my dad had just stopped existing. A fear that all my talking and thinking about Jesus and God and heaven amounted, in the end, to … nothing.'

'And did that feeling last?'

'Not like that, no. Not in that form. I got pretty warmed up to it all again, I had to or I'd have gone mad, but from the day he died until right now the gap has been just too wide.'

'Ah!' said Philip Hammond. 'Tell me about the gap.'

'You're going to think I'm very silly.'

'On the contrary, Martin, you appear quite sane to me, and I can assure you that I do know the difference. I meet some extraordinarily deluded people in the course of my work. And they are the saddest ones, those who have worked so hard on believing the lies they tell, that lies have become the only truth they know. So sad.'

I felt ridiculously pleased by this faint praise, but I couldn't see that it would help particularly. Sanity was not likely to be a primary qualification for heaven, was it?

'Tell me about the gap,' said Philip Hammond again.

'When I was a boy…' I began. I stopped as it suddenly occurred to me to wonder why that orange file of mine on the desk was so thin. Bit worrying. I'd ask in a minute. 'When I was a boy my brother and I spent a lot of time playing in the farmer's field just down the lane from where we lived. There was this wooded area at the bottom of the field, and in the middle of it there was a stream with steep banks sloping down to it on both sides. We used to pretend we were cowboys, and the idea was that we'd gallop our imaginary horses down the side of what we always called "the Grand Canyon", then leap majestically over the raging torrent beneath us. Well, my brother, who was a year or so older than me, with much longer legs, had no trouble with the "leaping majestically" part of the exercise. Over he went every single time, whooping loudly, and he'd land safely on the other side after almost every jump he did. One or two disasters, but they never seemed to put him off. He still operates in exactly the same way on the stock exchange now that he's supposed to be grown up.

'Me, though, I never wanted to jump over that stream. The raging torrent was actually a fairly mildly flowing brook, you understand, but the banks were quite high and there were a lot of angry-looking stones on the bed of that little stretch of water. I was terrified that I'd fall short of the opposite bank and hurt myself badly. I used to stand on one bank and measure the distance with my eye, and ask myself if I really thought I could reach the other side, even if I did my very best, best possible jump. And the answer was always that I couldn't. I knew I couldn't. It was just a couple of feet too wide for me to get across.

'My brother was always very good about it, mind you. We entered into a sort of unspoken agreement that my horse was temporarily lame, and needed to be led gently over the good old raging torrent using some stepping stones a few yards further down stream. He was good like that, my brother. Still is – was – is.'

'Is,' said Philip Hammond helpfully.

'Is, yes. Anyway, what I was going on to tell you was that after my father died I found myself, every now and then, slipping into an extraordinarily vivid daydream, a very silly daydream probably, but it says what I'm trying to say much better than I could. I still have it sometimes, especially when I'm not very confident. What happens is that I'm about ten years old again, grey shorts, knobbly knees and all, and I'm back at the top of the bank that sloped down to that stream where we played when I was young, and it's all more or less the way it used to be except that my brother isn't there, and I'm nervous – really nervous. Because I've sneaked down there on my own to prove to myself that, actually, I *can* do that frightening jump I've always chickened out of in the past. I'm jolly well *going* to do it, so that next time I'm down there with·my brother, I shall be able to go sailing over and amaze him.

'So there I am, and I get all revved up, and I clench my fists and gather up all my courage, and away I go running down the slope. But even as I'm racing along I find I'm measuring up the distance I'll have to cover to cross the raging trickle, and I can feel my legs slowing down, and I know nothing has changed. I'm not going to make it. And I never do. I screech to a halt when I reach the edge – just freeze, and feel like a silly failure all over again. The gap is too wide.

'And my problem with believing has been like that. It started at the moment when I saw my father looking so…so dead. I can't tell you how not-there he was, Philip. The gap between knowing what's true and real about the world and being alive – all the things you can see and feel and smell and whatever the other things you do with your senses are – the gap between that and believing there really is a heaven where individual people go on living and recognizing one another, and having the tears wiped from their eyes by God like the Bible says he's going to, is just too…'

I was quite glad to hear the telephone ring at that moment. I felt as if I could easily have got a bit carried away.

'Excuse me.'

Philip Hammond picked up the receiver and put it to his ear. I listened as he spoke quietly to the person on the other end.

'Yes?…Oh, yes…Excellent!…Yes, that would be just about right, we should be finished here fairly soon…Yes, I'm sure he will…No, not yet, but I'm quite sure the decision will be…Thank you…Yes, I will – goodbye.'

He placed the receiver gently down on its cradle and looked up at me, a little smile playing around his lips.

'Why is my file so thin?' I asked.

'Thin?' he said. 'Oh, well, just the most important things in here.' He picked up the orange folder and flicked through it again. 'Records of a few occasions when you've put yourself second – few but significant. And then, perhaps most importantly, there is the experience you had at six-thirty on October the fifteenth twenty-two years ago. Remember that?'

'My conversion, you mean?'

'I don't know if I'd call it that.'

Oh, dear.

'What would you call it, then?'

'It doesn't matter what I'd call it, Martin. The only thing that matters is that on that day you called out to Jesus and he heard you. He does also, as a matter of interest, hear some who, as far as they are aware, never did call out to him.'

'Philip,' I spoke in a very small voice, 'I did call out to him, and I did mean it, but – well, I don't think I love him as much as you're supposed…well, as much as everyone seemed to think you should really.'

'Oh, but Martin,' said Philip Hammond, with something that really did look suspiciously like a tear appearing in his eye, 'wait till you find out how much he loves you.'

A great shuddering sigh of hope and weariness passed through my entire being. 'So, you mean I'm…'

'You really do like to get hold of those little ready-made packets of truth, don't you? Aren't you interested to know who that was on the phone?'

'Am I allowed to know?'

'Certainly, it was your father.'

For a full thirty seconds I sat and stared at him. When I did speak at last it only felt safe to whisper. It was like those adventure stories where the trapped hero pulls a length of cotton with enormous care in order to grasp the length of string attached to it, which in turn is connected to the length of rope which is what he really needed in the first place. I didn't want to frighten this fragile possibility away.

'My father was speaking to you on the phone just then? *My father*? Are you seriously telling me that my father is…is somewhere near here? Alive, and near here?'

'Just through that door,' smiled Philip Hammond, indicating a door in the wall to the right of his desk that had certainly not been there when I first came into the office. 'You can go and see him now if you wish.'

I rose slowly from the chair I'd been occupying, my eyes fixed, wide and unblinking like a child's, on that insubstantial-looking wooden rectangle which, if this man was telling me the truth, was the only thing separating me from the person I loved so deeply and had so miserably feared was lost to me for ever.

'Just through that door?'

He gestured agreement with his arm. I didn't want to find out if he was right in case he wasn't. It took me an age to cross the room and actually take hold of the door handle. I turned back as something occurred to me.

'Is that it? Has the…is the assessment finished?'

'Almost. You carry on. I'll see you later.'

'Right – thanks. Thank you very much, err, Philip.'

Still I lingered. 'Tell me, is this normal procedure?'

'Normal procedure?'

I waved a hand vaguely around the room. 'All this. This office and the corridor and all the rest of it. Does this happen to everyone who comes through the…the system?'

'Every person is equally important,' he replied, 'but the things that are happening to you are…for you.'

'This isn't going to turn out to be a dream, is it?'

'Do you want to wake up, Martin, or do you want to go through that door and meet your father?'

'I…I want to meet my father.'

I wasn't actually aware of opening the door and passing through to the other side, but it seemed to happen in a trice. I was conscious only of hearing the door slam behind me, and the sudden impact of finding myself in a completely different and totally unexpected environment. The bright hope in my heart was switched off like a light bulb in a power-cut as I blinked and looked around, for a cruel joke had been played on me. Far from finding myself in an adjacent room as I had imagined would be the case, I had somehow been transported to the very scene that I had been describing to Philip Hammond just now. The door, the office, the grey corridor, the people I had met – all had disappeared without trace. Instead, when I turned my head, I saw the gently sloping field that had once been so familiar to me, its cattle-cropped grass reflecting that bright, motherly species of sunshine that always seemed to adorn Saturday mornings when I was a child. Before me, dropping away directly from where I stood, was the steep slope that led down to the stream where I had known my first real experience of failure. It was just as it had always been.

Where *was* my father? Why was I standing here, instead of seeing him as I had been promised? A sudden fear gripped me. Suppose I had, in fact, failed this assessment process, or whatever it was called, and the only way to get me out of the office was to promise me something I really wanted, so that I'd go without making a fuss? I gazed down the slope again. From where I was standing the stream looked wider than ever. What if Martin John Porter's bespoke hell was ordained to be an endless repetition of his failure to attempt the leap from one side of the raging torrent to the other? Eternal frustration and disappointment, together with the knowledge that I would be mocked perpetually by this glittering morning, so sweetly fragrant with hope. I shook my head slowly from side to side, longing to opt for the dream, hoping that it was still possible to refuse the fate that seemed to lie before me.

Only one thing possible.

Letting the weight of my body take me, I began to run before I had a chance to change my mind. I ran like the wind, managing to keep my balance only through a succession of small miracles, allowing gravity to carry me down the steep gradient with such exaggeratedly extended strides and at such a rate that I knew there was never going to be any question of stopping on the near side of the stream. I didn't want to. Even if it meant smashing on to those rocks at the speed I was travelling now, I didn't want to.

When my right foot thumped on to the turf at the edge of the nearest bank of the stream, I shut my eyes and pushed my whole self upwards and forwards with every ounce of strength that was left in me. When I opened them a split second later I saw, with a surge of pure joy, that my wild, last-ditch leap was indeed carrying me to the opposite bank of the raging torrent.

The other thing I saw in that eternally fulfilling moment was my father, his arms outstretched, waiting to steady me as I landed on the other side.

Friends Coming Round

'Doing anything tonight?'

'Depends what you mean by "anything". Fate has sentenced me to three hours of Ted Sewell. Good behaviour obligatory, but zero remission.'

On Friday the fifteenth of September at approximately three forty-five in the afternoon, whilst preparing to leave the toilet cubicle in which he had been absent-mindedly reading for a little longer than he needed to, Edward Sewell overheard these words. They marked the commencement of a brief conversation that was to result in him feeling very angry, deeply hurt, strangely excited, totally confused, and something else. The anger and hurt were because of what was said, and the excitement was because the contents of the conversation seemed to offer him an opportunity for the exercise of a kind of power he had never experienced before. The confusion was because of what happened afterwards. The something else was – something else.

The two people chatting out there by the urinals and the sinks were David Salmons, a crusty individual of near retirement age who headed up the maths department, and Michael Vinney, a man in his mid-thirties (Edward had just turned forty-three) who was a member of the Physical Education Department.

Salmons, a grey-haired, patched jacket of a man, whose verbal exchanges were famously saturated with growlingly cynical disappointment, had been at the school for years and years, and was reckoned, by common consent, to be a very good maths teacher and a very poor head of department. Those who served under him in the maths department were said to be looking forward to his departure at the end of the next school year with eager anticipation. Edward's relationship with Salmons had always been reasonably cordial but never more than distantly so. Valley Road Comprehensive was an extremely big school employing such a large number of staff that it was impossible to get to know more than a few of one's colleagues on anything but a superficial basis. Edward had nothing against Salmons – at least, he hadn't had until today.

Michael Vinney, on the other hand, was someone whom Edward knew well. Having begun at Valley Road on exactly the same day five years ago, they had been drawn together from time to time during those first few weeks by a common sense of temporary isolation in the staffroom, the occupants of which, at this early stage in their employment, suggested delegates to a convention of the less probable Dickensian characters.

Edward and Michael were different in almost every way you could imagine. Michael was not tall, but he was trimly fit and firm-bodied, a footballer and tennis player of real class, who, because of the uncompromising toughness of his approach, inspired enormous respect and a fair degree of loathing in most of his pupils, but didn't really care about the loathing as long as they did what they were told and worked hard to reach the limit of their potential. Children judged by him to have no potential simply ceased to exist in any meaningful way as far as P.E. was concerned. It was extremely rare for children to voice formal complaints about Mr Vinney's excesses, which were famous. He could be searingly sarcastic, and occasionally physically punitive, if the practice of hitting children can be described in that way, but somehow he seemed to carry with him such an unassailable right to do what he liked, that he got away with it every time.

On the only known occasion when a boy (Derek Williams in 3DL) had dared to protest to his parents about Mr Vinney clipping him round the ear for being lazy, Michael had survived by the performance of what, to outsiders, must have looked like an amazing conjuring trick. Derek's father turned up at the school to complain, but the P.E. teacher had been so forthright, matey and fulsomely flattering about the qualities of this boy who, it transpired, had far too much potential *not* to be clipped round the ear for the sake of his further development, that Mr Williams had shaken hands cordially with his son's attacker at the end of their meeting and gone home feeling that he had a real ally in the school. The boy himself, who may have been idle, but was certainly not stupid, must have realized that Mr Vinney had now, to all intents and purposes, been granted a licence to clip him round the ear whenever he saw fit. He wisely decided that discretion was the better part of valour, relocating his laziness to the lessons of another, less divinely protected teacher. Derek's father, deeply impressed by the subsequent dramatic improvement in his son's achievements in P.E., declared to anyone who cared to listen that he personally wouldn't hear a word said against Mr Vinney's methods, because, when all was said and done, they worked!

Michael's body, his desk, his routine and his approach to the world were about as ordered and unvaried as it was possible for such things to be. Practical as well as sporty, he was good at making things and mending things. He understood cars and drove them very fast and skilfully.

Michael had only one weakness that Edward knew about. His Achilles heel was situated, as Edward was fond of saying silently to himself, on his head. He was losing his hair, and he didn't like it. All that remained as he approached his thirty-sixth birthday was a light, furry down which, though distributed fairly evenly over the surface of his scalp, was very thin indeed and getting thinner by every baby-shampoo wash. Michael had never actually expressed this concern to Edward, but his wife, Sophie, had mentioned it (in the strictest confidence – Mike would kill her if he thought anyone knew he got worked up about such a silly vain thing, especially if they knew how many times a day she, Sophie, had to reassure him that it didn't really notice) to Edward's wife, Jenny, who had meant exactly what she said, but it had been her habit ever since getting married to mentally exclude Edward from the universe of souls she would never tell, whenever she made that promise. There had to be someone you could tell everything to, didn't there? Besides, Edward would never tell anyone else, so it didn't matter, did it?

Edward was tall, dressed by a committee, more than a little overweight (cuddly, Jenny said), totally impractical, about as sporty as a melting snowman, and blessed with a fine head of thick, dark-brown, usually dishevelled hair. He was an English teacher (mainly for the money nowadays) who really only wanted to be allowed to read books, drink fine wine and eat good food with his wife and friends, go to France and be a poet. Mr Sewell's vagueness and whimsicality in school were so pronounced for most of the time he spent in the classroom that he should have been taken apart by the children he taught. Occasionally he was. But Edward displayed such a genuine and unusual intensity of appreciative interest in the words and works of his pupils, combined with the most confusingly straight-faced irony when the situation warranted it, that most classes seemed to have made a sort of unconscious, corporate decision that there was more to be gained from listening and observing than from misbehaving.

On one occasion, for instance, not long after arriving at Valley Road, Edward had been teaching a notorious fourth-year class, newly elevated from their position as a notorious third-year class. Such classes tend to put a lot of hard work into maintaining their notoriety and this class was certainly no exception. Just after the lesson had begun, a boy called Jackson Ford, who was unofficially responsible for organizing nuisance artillery from the back row, started waggling a stiff arm in the air with all the agitation of an infant urgently needing to go to the toilet.

'Yes, Jackson?' enquired Edward, laying down *A Passage To India*, from which he had been reading the final couple of pages, and giving the boy his entire, fascinated attention. 'What would you like to say to me?'

'Walker and me, Sir,' gesturing towards the grinning youth on his left, 'we're finding this stuff you're reading really boring, and we thought, if it's all the same to you, Sir, we'd take a stroll out to the grass over there and have a smoke until the lesson ends.'

Naturally, delighted laughter greeted this piece of calculated insolence, and all eyes turned to Mr Sewell, each face silently asking that most deliciously anticipatory question of all: 'What are you going to do about that, Teacher?'

Edward seemed genuinely puzzled for a moment, simply because he actually was, then his brow cleared and an expression of bright enthusiasm appeared on his face.

'I wonder,' he said, 'if you could really bring yourself to do that. Most interesting! Here am I, an ordinary, tweedy, conventional schoolmaster who is employed to teach English Literature to, among others, you, Jackson, and here are you, an average to bright fourth-year pupil who is supposed to learn the English Literature that I am supposed to teach. It sounds like a glorious convergence, doesn't it Jackson?' Jackson evinced no desire to offer an opinion. 'But Messrs Fielding and Aziz could tell us how misleading it is possible for such an assumption to be, could they not? How might we both cope with the situation if I were to agree to your request, flippant though I know that request to have been?' He glanced invitingly around the class. 'Perhaps somebody would care to map out for us the trail of consequences that would have its starting point in that agreement. How, for instance, would the headmaster react, on glancing up from his desk, to the sight of Jackson Ford quietly smoking his way through second lesson out on the playing field? What would his response be to the news that he was there with my permission? William Styles, would you care to come out here and be the headmaster, asking me what on earth I think I'm playing at, and Gillian, might you offer us a convincing impression of Jackson struggling to decide whether to take the blame himself or to shop me?'

Jackson Ford, thoroughly bewildered by this experience of seeing his deliberate rudeness turned into the basis of some sort of academic debate and class role-play, found it quite impossible to work out whether Mr Sewell was taking the mickey, or whether he was just loony. Unable to come down firmly on one side or another, he decided to lie low in English for a little while. He spent quite a lot of his lying-low time in chewing over the suggestion that he was 'average to bright'. He'd thought he was no more than average…

Friendships that have their origins in the loneliness and insecurity of a new situation can become rather laboured later on and perhaps peter out, as those involved find their feet and discover that they have other, more interesting things in common with people who seemed quite intimidating in those first dank days. This, Edward considered, might well have happened with himself and Michael if it had not been for two major factors.

First, the two wives got on extremely well. Michael had invited Edward and his wife to a meal within a week of the two men first meeting, and Sophie and Jenny had taken to each other immediately.

Sophie, eight years younger than her husband, was one of those chatty, good-natured, pretty, pert-bottomed girls who appear to live in a constant state of surprise and alarm over the fact that age and parenthood have relentlessly press-ganged them into the ranks of the grown-ups. The upbringing of her two-year-old boy, Paul, obviously occasioned her the most alarm. Sophie adored Paul, but seemed to regard him as a sort of human crossword puzzle provided without the benefit of clues. Meeting Jenny, whose sons, David and Stephen, were fourteen and ten years old respectively, had been a great comfort to her. From the beginning she had confided recklessly in the older woman, finding in Jenny a quiet, motherly stability that allowed her opportunities once more safely to be the little girl that she was secretly quite sure she always had been and always would be in reality.

Jenny, for her part, enjoyed Sophie's bright, wide-eyed garrulousness and was quite happy, when it was needed, to take a maternal role in her friend's life. Paul was as enchanting and exhausting as only two-year olds can be. It was a pleasure to offer at least a couple of clues to help fill in the crossword. Apart from anything else, Jenny had never really had what Edward called a 'shrieking with laughter' relationship with another woman before. It wasn't her style, in any case. With Sophie, though, she rather enjoyed the explosions of raucousness that sometimes erupted from the silliest of jokes and situations, often over the sink, for some peculiar reason. Edward said that she must have missed out on some crucially character-building 'raucous phase' in her teenage years, and that it was good to catch up now.

The other major factor in the continuance of the friendship between Edward and Michael was, in Edward's view, the mutual discovery that both of them had been heavily involved at one time in problems connected with what they had both referred to in their early discussions as 'churchgoing'. Michael was obviously not very practised in the business of opening up about himself, but he did tell Edward and Jenny that part of his story in some detail.

Michael's parents had been life-long Pentecostals of the devout but unquestioning variety, who not only expected to remain faithful to Christ until their dying day, but automatically assumed that their only son would follow suit, especially as, to their great satisfaction, he had made his own personal commitment to Jesus when he was a little boy of only seven.

Within days of leaving home to train as a P.E. teacher, Michael told himself that he now knew for sure something he had suspected for a long time, namely, that none of the things his parents believed so committedly had made a real home in his own heart. He struggled quite hard for a little while to make appropriate things happen inside himself, but it was a waste of time. He was definitely not a Christian, he decided. So troubled was he, though, by the prospect of telling his fond mother and father that he was atheistic in his views, that he maintained the pretence of sharing their beliefs for as long as they both lived, attending church when he was at home just as he had always done, singing, praying out loud occasionally, and even raising his hands during the worship as most of the others did.

When both of his parents were killed in a motorway accident two years after he qualified, Michael experienced an odd mixture of pain and relief. The pain was because he loved them and knew he would miss them. He was relieved because, by the very nature of the accident, he could safely assume that their deaths must have been instantaneous, and they had gone together. There would be no loneliness in old age for either of them. And there would be no further need for him to pretend anything about God. There was no God. All that was finished.

Edward's story was similar in one important sense, though very different in others. He had been brought up by his widowed father, an immensely kind, quiet man, who passed his passionate love for books and ideas on to Edward and his older sister, Sandra, a university lecturer, now married and resident in Western Australia with her husband and two daughters.

The similarity between Edward and Michael lay in the fact that Edward's father had also been a devout Christian, although he had not followed the Pentecostal tradition. A life-long and fairly traditional Anglican, he would have felt uncomfortable in the more emotional ethos of the kind of church in which Michael had grown up. Nevertheless, his faith was as important to him as his children were, and he prayed diligently every morning that one day both Edward and Sandra would come to know and love Jesus as he did. Unlike Michael's parents, however, he was a clear-eyed realist, and a man who valued integrity in himself and others. He was perfectly aware that, although Edward had certainly followed him in his love for literature, and his joy in the exercise of mind and spirit, he had not inherited a passion for the Christian faith or the person of Jesus, and he would have hated the very idea of his son feeling obliged to pretend otherwise. Sandra and her husband and family had become very involved members of a big, lively church in the city of Perth, something for which he thanked God daily, but Edward remained a warmly affectionate, amiable agnostic, a clear target for the power of persistent, faithful prayer, as far as his father was concerned.

Edward greatly respected his father's religious views, and, if it had been at all possible, would gladly have embraced them himself, but he explained that he simply could not find a sufficiently good reason to sacrifice exploration of all the possible horizons of thought and feeling that might appear, to a God who would probably want to fence his mind off into very prescribed and spiritually disinfected little paddocks of inner experience. In vain, on the occasions when he said this, his father offered the mild suggestion that Edward might be reacting to his image of the Church rather than to the actual nature of God. But Edward would just grin and shake his head and say, 'Don't think so, Pop,' and go and make a pot of tea before getting the Scrabble out.

When this happened the old man smiled and nodded, but he never gave up praying.

Edward's father lived well into his eighties and died in considerable discomfort from cancer not long after Edward and Jenny's youngest, Stephen, was born. Jenny and her father-in-law had become very close during the fifteen years that they had known each other, and it was she who had been more than willing to nurse him through the final weeks of his life.

Edward had wonderful memories of his father, but there was one recollection in particular that caused him excruciating pain whenever it rose, always unbidden, to the front of his mind.

One Saturday morning in the middle of summer, not long before the old fellow became ill, Edward and Jenny and the boys had decided to drive up into the hills with the dog and take a good long walk. Edward's father had elected to stay at home and do a spot of very slow 'pottering', as he called it, around Jenny's beloved garden.

After successfully shovelling everybody into the car and setting off, Edward, who was driving, suddenly remembered that although they definitely had one large and very excited dog with them, he had forgotten to take the dog's lead from the hook by the front door. Encounters with other dogs sometimes urgently required the lead to be available, so he pulled up at the end of the road, and walked quickly back towards the house. Letting himself in through the front door, he grabbed the lead, and was about to call out reassuringly, when he heard the sound of a voice coming from the kitchen. It was his father, speaking in passionately imploring tones.

'...and heavenly father, I know you always listen to me, and I'm so grateful to you for that and so many prayers answered in my life. I'm ... well, it's been such a privilege and a joy knowing you, it really has, but...' The elderly, wheezing voice broke a little as it continued. 'I bring my beloved Edward before you yet again, Lord, knowing that you love him more than I do. Grant my dearest wish, and draw him and his family to you when the right time comes. I beg you, Lord, in your great kindness, to hear my prayer...'

Edward stole out with the lead, closing the door carefully and soundlessly behind him as he went. He dashed the moisture angrily from his eyes as he walked back to the car. He knew that his father prayed daily for his conversion, but he had never actually heard him doing it before. It seemed so sad and unfair that he couldn't give his father the thing he wanted most in the world. But he couldn't. He simply couldn't lie to his father, and his father would have known he wasn't telling the truth anyway. Blast!

Edward didn't use words like 'Blast'.

Over the years the memory of that painful moment in the hall, when he had discovered the surprising depth of passion in his father's relationship with a God who didn't exist, had become like a slight but chronic physical pain, ever liable to start aching and throbbing when other concerns and distractions faded for a while.

It was on the second occasion that the Sewells and the Vinneys ate together, this time at the solid, four-bedroomed Victorian house in Oxford Avenue that Edward had inherited from his father, that Michael, still feeling new and vulnerable, had talked quite freely about his parents and his 'churchgoing' background. Edward said afterwards to Jenny that he felt Michael had offered this very personal piece of information as a sort of deposit of disclosure into a relationship account that he desperately needed to keep open at that time. Accustomed to such convoluted metaphors, she understood and agreed.

Jenny had been quite surprised on that same evening to hear Edward responding with a detailed description of his own experiences with his father, including the business of the overheard prayer. You were supposed to be careful with pearls, weren't you? Not, of course, she hastily added to herself, that Michael and Sophie were swine. That was not what she'd meant at all.

Invitations to dinner continued to be exchanged on a regular basis after that. Jenny and Sophie always enjoyed these occasions, having become really good friends. They also met for morning coffee and cake almost every week, usually at Sophie's house because of it being easier with Paul, chatting about their children and the jobs they'd done and their houses and what the future might hold. Sophie talked quite a lot about Michael, who, as Jenny soon began to realize, remained more or less in pedagogic mode in his dealings with the pretty, ingenuous girl whom he had married. Jenny made the occasional remark about Edward, but, like her husband, she had never felt the need or inclination to share intimate details of their married life, and there was no temptation to start doing so now.

For Edward, the ongoing relationship between himself and Michael was much more problematical. He was well aware that, since the time when they had both joined the staff group, Michael had gained a great deal of confidence, and a set of friends from among the other teachers who were his own age, and with whom he had much more in common. They tended to be a fairly brash, sporty bunch, who enjoyed beer in large quantities (Edward was all for alcohol, but he and Jenny infinitely preferred the grape to the hop) and spoke loudly in the staffroom about how horrible most of the the boys were and how much they fancied some of the girls. When Edward told Jenny about this she asked him if he had ever fancied any of the girls, and laughed when he said, yes, almost all of the sixth form, and particularly Elsie Warningham.

In a sense Edward felt protective towards his friend, or rather, he felt that, in that early exchange of experiences, he had tacitly accepted a responsibility to safeguard a part of Michael that could easily fade and disappear in the company of those with whom he now spent most of his leisure time. He was not always sure about Michael's attitude towards him, but he hoped and believed that one important aspect of his young colleague's personality was fed and nurtured by this periodic exposure to a deeper, more abstract and poetic view of life. Every now and then, he would deliberately bring up the subject of their contrasting religious backgrounds in order to, as it were, re-establish the stamp of their conversational currency. Whenever he did this Michael would listen and nod attentively, apparently thinking very seriously about what was being said, even if he himself tended to say less and less on the subject as time went by.

Edward was certainly a good man, and essentially a humble one, but he had perhaps never quite caught on to the fact that he was slightly unusual, and that other people might not be as enchanted or absorbed by the prospect of sharing his thoughts and fancies as he imagined.

On hearing those initial, devastating lines of dialogue issuing with such clarity from the other side of the toilet door, Edward's first and most automatic reaction was a feeling that he should cover his ears. The voice of his rather old-fashioned upbringing told him that a gentleman does not listen to other people's private conversations, and that, if he does, he certainly should not expect to hear good of himself. But, good heavens above, it was too late for that! Michael's blistering reply to the other man's question had hit him like a punch in the throat before he was given any choice about whether to listen or not. As he absorbed the full impact of what he had just heard, Edward, who was, after all, a perfectly normal human being in most ways, knew that he was no more capable of deliberately blocking out whatever was still to come than he was capable of flying to the moon. He remained perfectly still and listened.

'Thought he was a friend of yours,' he heard Salmons say.

'More of a barnacle on my backside,' replied Michael. 'My own stupid fault. When I first came I was a bit new and green and whatnot, so I latched on to the first human being who'd pass the time of day with me.'

'And you couldn't find a human being so you settled for the resident loony, eh?'

'All my life,' Michael's voice was affectedly weary, 'I seem to have got sucked in by the village idiot whenever I go somewhere new. Must be something about me that appeals to them, I suppose.'

'Best English teacher this school's ever had,' said Salmons, reflectively and rather unexpectedly. He returned to the topic in hand, his voice droningly flat and dismissive. 'I should just cool it off, if I were you. Surely you don't have to spend time with the man if you don't want to, do you? I wouldn't. Three hours of purgatory on a Friday night. What's the point if you're not even a Catholic?'

The two men must have moved away from the urinals at this point. First one tap was turned on and then another. Edward, now in a strange, light-headed state, found himself wondering irrelevantly whether either of the teachers would have bothered washing their hands if the other one hadn't been there. He leaned forward, straining to hear what was said over the noise of water rushing into the sinks.

'The trouble is,' Michael raised his voice as if to oblige, 'we're stuck in one of those blasted "you come to dinner with us, and then we'll come to dinner with you, and then you come to dinner with us" things that go on and on until you emigrate or die. I don't know how to get out of it. I wouldn't...' He dropped his volume as the sound of the running taps ceased. 'Sorry – didn't mean to shout. I wouldn't want to actually upset the old idiot. I suppose he can't help being a chop short of a mixed grill. Besides, Sophie really likes going there and them coming to us – gets on like a house on fire with Mrs Loony. Jenny's all right, actually. Got a lot of time for her. Poor cow.'

One of them had turned on the hot air machine.

'I'll tell you the thing I really can't stand.' Michael was really warming to his theme now. 'Every time we have one of these joyful little gatherings – well, nearly every time – old Sewell seems to feel obliged to go back to stuff we talked about years ago, personal stuff I wish I'd never said.'

'What sort of personal stuff?'

For the first time an evasive note sounded in Michael's voice.

'Aah, just things that happened, you know. I think he thinks we've got some kind of special bond, or something. Reckons it gives him a sort of hold over me. Teach me to keep my mouth shut, won't it?'

'Will it?' whispered Edward involuntarily, but very softly to himself inside his cubicle.

'Still,' continued Michael, as the sound of the hand-drier stopped then started again, 'I suppose I should be thankful for small mercies. At least when he's doing that he's not drifting off into "What if this?" and "What if that?" and "Let's tease out what we actually mean when we describe somebody as a creative person". That was one of his merrier suggestions at the last wake we held. Then, of course, there's "Would you be interested in hearing a line or two of the verse I've been working on?" Mustn't forget that one. If ever he publishes a collection of poems it'll have to be called *Look At My Entrails*. Boy! What I wouldn't give sometimes for a verse or two of "Eskimo Nell" and ten minutes on whether United are going to win the league.'

'I don't think you'd enjoy dinner with me any more than you do with him,' observed Salmons drily, 'not that I shall ever ask you, I hasten to add. My devoted staff would pin you to the ground behind the bikesheds the following morning and force you to divulge my darkest secrets. Not that you'd take much forcing, of course.'

'What makes you say that?'

After the door to the staff toilet block had squeaked open and slammed shut, Edward could still hear the maths teacher's crackling laugh echoing derisively down the corridor outside.

For quite a long time after the two men had gone Edward remained virtually motionless inside the cubicle, focusing his eyes on a small jagged mark near the centre of the green-painted chipboard door in front of him. He was trying to get his breathing under control. For the last few minutes, ever since that conversation had begun, in fact, hardly any air had passed in or out of his lungs. He had never felt quite like this before in his life. It was like being beaten up, as though someone had climbed right into your head wearing boxing gloves and pummelled your brain mercilessly in the places where it was most tender. Bruises everywhere.

Waves of anger and humiliation and hurt began to wash around inside his chest and stomach, making him feel sick with the need for comfort and a chance to hit back. To believe that you were helping, and then to discover that you were being tolerated – patronized! He wanted to see his wife, who wouldn't be back from the hospital just yet, and he wanted to see his sons, who were away on camp, and he wanted to see his father, who was dead. He even felt a sudden painful desire to see his mother, of whom he had no memory at all. He felt about six years old.

'Baldy!' he hissed at the door through gritted teeth. 'I hate you, Baldy! Baldy, Baldy, Baldy, Baldy! I hate you, Mr Michael Baldy Not Much Hair Going Bald And Doesn't Like It Baldy Vinney!'

The sound of someone coming in through the outer door cut short this very necessary release of Edward's overflow of aggression, turning it instead into a quite frightening attack of breathlessness. For two or three minutes he gasped as silently as he could into a handkerchief held in his cupped hands, praying that whoever had come in would hurry up and do whatever they'd come to do, and then clear off.

Able to come out at last a short while later, rather shaky and still battling a little for breath, he leaned, stiff-armed, with his hands on the sides of one of the wash-basins, studying his strained, frowning face in the mirror for a moment. There had always been a detached element in Edward's personality that was not just able to, but almost always did, regard all the things that happened to him, however negative or traumatic, as *interesting*, in exactly the same way that Jackson Ford's deliberate act of disruption was an *interesting* thing to observe and contemplate.

'And what are you going to do with all this, Edward Sewell?' he asked his reflection. 'Are you going to confront Michael down in the staffroom in a moment and tell him that you know what he really thinks about you and your dinner parties and your conversation and your poetry and your poor cow of a wife?'

He tried to picture Michael, horrified beyond measure, at the moment when it was revealed to him that all those scathing comments had been listened to by the last person he would ever have wanted to hear them. What sort of flustered, blundering attempts would he make to justify the horrible things that he'd said?

'Oh, n-o-o-o! You didn't think I meant it, did you? Oh, you didn't! I was just having old Salmons on – giving him something to be really miserable about.'

'I knew you were there all the time! Ha! Caught you there, didn't I? Been waiting to see how long it was before you said something…'

'Actually, Ted, I haven't been all that well for the last few days, a bit down about some private things as well as some kind of virus – I've been in a funny state of mind. Don't take any notice of what I said, it doesn't mean a thing. Maybe we could have a chat about this private stuff sometime – if that's all right with you, I mean…'

Yes, indefensible though his behaviour might have appeared, Michael wouldn't be flustered and blundering at all. He would be bound to come out with something pretty impressive in the way of an excuse. He was famous for it at Valley Road. Probably, by the time he'd finished, Edward would be humbly apologizing for putting their friendship in jeopardy by making such a silly fuss about nothing. Michael would, no doubt, be big enough to accept his apology with good grace.

'In any case,' he argued to his reflection, 'things you say about people when they aren't there haven't necessarily got much at all to do with what you really think about them. You just say things to sound clever, or to fit in with the way you think the person you're talking to feels about things. Or you only mean the horrible stuff that comes out a little bit, but it gets kind of blown up on the way out. Perhaps Michael was just exaggerating. Everyone does that, don't they?'

No, they don't, replied Edward silently to himself, as the burning anger rose once more like bile in his throat, they don't talk like Michael did just now, slicing and crushing and contemptuously flicking from their perfect cuffs, like specks of dust, all the things that mean so much to somebody else. Not when they've been friends, they don't. Not to someone else who's quite likely to pass it all on to the rest of the crowd. No, not everyone does that.

Michael had done, done, *done* it, and a part of Edward that rarely became roused was burning to do something to him in return. His dark thoughts turned to the dinner party planned for seven o'clock that same evening. Perhaps he should just cancel it — tell Michael and Sophie he was sick, or had to go somewhere. Even as he considered that option, though, a new aspect of the situation occurred to him, and the more he thought about it, the more a different and really quite pleasant sensation began to creep over him. The fact was that he knew what Michael thought about him now, but Michael had no idea that he knew. How interesting to observe events from the vantage point of possessing that extra information. Perhaps, thought Edward, it might not be such a bad evening after all.

Downstairs, in the crowded, noisy staffroom, Michael was in the act of lifting his coat from a peg by the door as Edward walked in. He raised a hand in greeting.

'Okay, Ted? What a week, eh? Time to set the animals on the general public and close the zoo for a couple of days. All systems go for seven o'clock?'

Taken aback by the sheer normalness of Michael-the-Enemy's manner towards him, Edward was unable to speak for a second or two. How could this person who was smiling and joking with him now be the same person who had said all those horrible things ten minutes ago? Feeling suddenly cold and confused, he found himself just wanting the whole thing to go away.

'I ... I was thinking, Michael – if you get home and suddenly wish you could simply flop instead of spending the whole evening with someone you already see all week as it is, you've only got to give me a ring and we can...you know, reorganize it. I don't want you to feel – what would the word be? – bound. I would hate you to feel bound.'

Michael froze for a moment, one arm in the left sleeve of his coat, the other poised in mid-quest for the one behind his back. He peered at Edward with narrow-eyed, exaggerated anxiety.

'Are you on something, Edward? Tannin, is it? You've got to watch that school tea, you know. Easy to overdose without realizing you're doing it. What *are* you talking about? I wouldn't miss one of our little get-togethers for anything. Nor would Sophie – you know that.' He paused for an instant. 'Look, is it that you'd rather we didn't come tonight, because...'

'Oh, no!' Edward interrupted hurriedly, suddenly seeing Jenny's face in his mind's eye for some reason. He moved forward to help Michael into his coat. 'No, it's just that it occurred to me...well, we fix a date for these things quite a long way in advance, don't we, and we ought to, as it were, include a back-out clause, just in case either of us wants to err, you know, back out, or...'

Turning, Michael laid a leather-gloved hand on his arm and spoke with mock gravity.

'Edward, we're coming to dinner, not buying your house. Of course we want to come round. What are we having by the way? I've starved myself all day ready for tonight's do.'

The anger surfaced again. Get your hand off my arm!

'Err, I'm not sure – I think it might be mixed grill, that is, assuming we can get the chops without any trouble. I mean, it wouldn't be a mixed grill without a chop, would it? I don't think it would.'

'Without a…no, no, I suppose not.' Michael scratched his head in bafflement. 'Look, if I were you, Ted, I'd go home, have quite a sizeable scotch and take it easy for an hour or two. All right? I think you must have overdone it this week. Oh, by the way, there's something serious I want you and I to have a talk about this evening after dinner, if that's okay. See you at seven. Love to Jenny. Cheers!'

'Something you want to…?'

But Michael had gone, leaving Edward wishing devoutly that his ridiculous comment about the mixed grill could be expunged from the history of the world, and feeling in an even greater state of confusion than before. Why should Michael want to discuss anything serious with the barnacle on his backside – the village idiot – the boring holder of wakes? The whole of the encounter he had just endured didn't seem to fit anywhere with the conversation he had overheard – not just in terms of words, but in terms of…well, of heart. The Staffroom Michael wasn't the Toilet-block Michael at all. They just weren't the same person. For one irrational moment, Edward really did wonder if he'd got it all wrong and it had been someone else out there talking to Salmons. But he knew he hadn't. He jolly well hadn't got it wrong. It had been Michael, and Michael was coming to dinner tonight.

Driving his battered Volvo home through the busily crowded early darkness of the market town where he lived, Edward changed his mind at least five times about whether to tell his wife what had happened or not. That she would know perfectly well *something* had happened was in no doubt at all. Edward was transparent at the best of times, and Jenny was able to read every one of his moods like themes in a favourite book. He would either have to tell her the truth, or invent something to account for his jittery state. A nasty headache might be the answer. He did actually suffer from them when he was tired sometimes, and a headache was vague enough to account for all sorts of unusual behaviour. He'd have to tell her what had really happened in the end, of course. He'd burst otherwise.

As he pulled off the High Street and turned right into Oxford Avenue, Edward asked himself why he was (temporarily, at any rate) unwilling to share what had happened with Jenny. He usually told her everything as soon as it happened. Two reasons sprang to mind.

The first was a reluctance to ignite one of his wife's occasional, awesome rages. Jenny was quite capable of getting very cross indeed, especially when she felt that her husband was under attack or being treated unfairly. She might – she just might – go straight to the phone and cancel tonight's dinner party using that tight, incensed voice that had always spoilt Edward's day on the rare occasions when it was directed at him. He was pretty sure now that he didn't want the evening to be cancelled. Under the circumstances, the prospect of being with Michael and a couple of bottles of wine for three or four hours on home ground was nerve-racking but...well, *interesting*. Knowledge certainly did feel as if it might be power. Edward had never really given much thought to the general concepts of having or exercising power before.

The other reason for not telling Jenny had more to do with her wisdom than her rage. In this second scenario she might not cancel the evening, and, in a way, that would be even worse. Edward was virtually certain that once his wife's anger had abated she would begin to take a mature, adult view of the situation. If she hadn't made the cancelling phone-call by the time that inevitable abating stage arrived, he was sure she would express a carefully considered opinion that the dinner should go ahead, and then offer lots of sensible observations about the unfairness of blaming Sophie for Michael's silliness, and the inadvisibility of giving overmuch credence to accidentally overheard remarks, and the fact that the truly grown-up and constructive mode of response was to carry on as if nothing had happened. If the evening proceeded on that basis Edward wouldn't be able to enjoy any sense of secret knowledge or subtle power. Nor would it be possible to manufacture opportunities to taste the (to him) hitherto virtually unknown flavour of revenge, a concept that Edward had thought even less about in the course of his life than he'd thought about power. The mature approach scorned revenge. Jenny would kick him under the table if she saw any sign of it.

As he parked a little way up the avenue to leave his drive clear for Michael's Daewoo, or whatever it was called, later on, Edward made a final decision. He wouldn't tell Jenny tonight, he'd tell her tomorrow, and that was absolutely definite – probably.

Jenny called out from the kitchen as he shut the front door against the cold evening outside. Good! She was back early.

'Good day, love? I can't believe we've got a whole weekend without the boys. Haven't forgotten we've got the Vinneys tonight, have you? You need to put the car up the road, don't you?'

'Done it,' called back Edward in a headache-weakened voice as he hung his coat on the rack in the hall. 'Seems a shame when there's just us for once.'

Jenny was chopping vegetables when he walked into the kitchen. Such a comfortable, familiar figure, thought

Edward for the ten thousandth time. A warm and glowing armful. Not a skinny bird. The other day she'd been quite flattered when he told her that she reminded him of the lady who did the Bisto adverts on television. She turned to look at him, her always sympathetic brown eyes registering slight concern.

'You all right, Edward? You sound a bit woozy. What – d'you mean you wish they weren't coming?'

'Bit of a headache – nothing much. No, not really – no, it'll be fine. Besides, Michael says he's got something important he wants to talk about.'

'To us?'

'Me. Don't know what it is.'

'Oh, pardon me for existing, I'm sure. Intriguing. Something to do with the blessed job I expect. Ah, well, Sophie and me'll polish off what's left of the Baileys in the kitchen while you're talking about something important over your brandy glasses. She certainly won't mind. Nor will I. You can tell me what it was afterwards.' She studied his face for a second or two. 'You sure it's just a headache?'

For a moment Edward stood stiffly, his body swaying very slightly. He came very close to blurting out everything that had happened. To see Jenny's eyes darken with anger on his behalf; to immerse his bruised feelings in the warm stream of sympathy that would undoubtedly pour from her spirit to his when she heard the ghastly details; to hear her say how unfair she thought it was to talk like that about someone who was supposed to be your friend; all these things would have been most welcome and enjoyable. He resisted the temptation.

'Mmm, had it all day. I'll take some pain-killers. Shall I do the table? And then I'll have my shower.'

'Please. I'll carry on with the dinner and put your tablets in some squash. I got the wine, so you can open that ready, too.'

After carefully laying the table in the dining-room and uncorking the two bottles of red wine that he found on top of the bureau, Edward went upstairs for a shower, then came back down from his bedroom with a large pad of writing-paper and a Biro. Pulling one of the dining-room chairs away from the table, he sat with one leg crossed over the other, staring into the distance and frowning with concentration as he sucked the end of his pen. After a few minutes he took a determinedly deep breath through his nose, straightened the pad on his knee and began to write. So absorbed was he by this task, that Jenny had to call out to him twice that his dissolved headache tablets were still waiting for him in the kitchen.

'Unless, of course,' she added after the second time, 'you haven't got it any more...'

By the time the ring on the doorbell came at one minute past seven, Edward had finished his piece of writing, and was in a state of considerable tension. He felt as if he was about to take the leading role in some highly dramatic piece of theatre, but without the benefit of knowing what his lines were to be, or how the other characters in the play were scheduled to speak or behave or react to him. What about Sophie? Did she know what her husband really thought of his 'loony' colleague? What a farce it would all seem if she did.

Whether or not Sophie was privy to Michael's views on Edward, there was little doubt that she was pleased to have arrived that evening. She was the first to trip her way over the doorstep and into the house when Edward answered the bell.

'Eddeee!'

She pecked him brightly on the cheek, dumped her coat with comfortable familiarity over the newel post at the bottom of the stairs, and tottered happily down the hall in her high heels, rather like, thought Edward, a Thelwell pony walking on its hind legs. She really did have calves that were almost edible. Even before entering the kitchen she was beginning to emit the shrill, anticipatory scream with which she invariably greeted Jenny. A moment later Edward heard his wife's deeper, more relaxed laugh sounding in response.

Michael too was all smiles and laid-back familiarity, the very picture of a man at ease finding himself in a place where he was genuinely able to relax. He placed the statutory gift of wine on the hall table.

'Believe this or not, Ted,' he said, as Edward took his coat and scarf and swivelled to hang them on the rack, 'but stepping through this front door of yours makes me feel more at home than just about anything else I know.' As Edward turned back from the coat-rack Michael seized his hand and squeezed it firmly. 'I really mean that.'

What?

For the first time Edward was able to understand what people meant when they talked about being struck dumb. He clutched Michael's hand and stared into his face, completely unable to speak. For goodness' sake! How could the man's voice communicate such engaging intimacy? How did he manage to make his eyes do the warm, crinkly, deeply sincere thing that he was making them do now? How could he possibly have meant what he said earlier if what he was saying now was as genuine as it seemed to be? Aware suddenly that his mouth was hanging open, he shook his head slightly and cast desperately about in his mind for some kind of reply. The result was not, he felt, inspired.

'You do?'

Michael burst into laughter.

'Well, there's no need to sound quite so surprised, mate.' He called loudly down the hall. 'Jenny! This husband of yours is amazed because I said that I like coming here very much. Just shows how clever he is, because I was actually lying through my teeth.' He laughed loudly again.

Edward's polite but feebly expressed protestations that he hadn't meant that at all were lost in a corresponding chorus of laughter from Jenny and Sophie as they emerged from the kitchen with glasses in their hands. He tried to join in, but was conscious of only being able to manage a sickly grin and a vague croaking noise in the back of his throat.

'Anyway,' breezed Michael, 'assuming Sophie and I can bear to stay for just a little longer, there are three things that have to be done right now. First, I have to give the beautiful Jennifer a kiss…'

He did so. Edward balled his fists, but kept them by his sides. Huh! Right! Wanted to kiss the poor cow, did he? Thought she might like to find out how it felt to be kissed by someone normal, perhaps?

Sophie smiled happily at everybody and sipped her drink.

'The second thing is to ask how you two ladies have managed to get into the booze within seconds of us coming through the front door, whereas we men are so nearly dead of thirst that you probably wouldn't be able to prise our poor parched lips open far enough to get a little moisture in even if you wanted to. Eh, Ted?'

Edward, who found 'chaps and girls' talk difficult at the best of times, forced a smile on to his face and nodded miserably. Light banter was the last thing he felt capable of at the moment. He studied Michael's hair, taking comfort from the sparseness of it. It really was very thin. He realized he should be saying something to Michael, but he couldn't think of anything. Jenny did, thank goodness.

'Ah, well, you see,' she replied playfully, 'it's like this, Michael. I already had a drink, which, as the author of the coming feast, I might add, I've hardly had a chance to touch, so the bottle was already out on the kitchen table. Add the fact that Sophie knows where the glasses are, and that she's got more sense than to wait for me to get round to inviting her, and there you are. We've got drinks and you haven't.' She winked at Sophie and pursed her lips as if debating inwardly. 'What do you think? Shall we let them have one?'

Wrinkling her nose and tilting her head, Sophie closed one eye and stared up at the light-fitting on the hall ceiling with the other, portraying serious thought like a bad actor.

'Yes!' she announced finally. 'Yeah, if they're good we'll let 'em 'ave one.'

More laughter. Ha ha!

'Speaking of the coming feast,' continued Michael, 'the third thing I have to do is to say that…'

'Are you going to offer Michael a drink, Edward? Sorry, Michael, I just thought you ought to have something to brace you before you do your third thing. I don't know how clever people like you do it. They do it on television don't they? "There are three points I would like to make in this context." I've never been able to think in threes.'

Edward picked up his cue obediently, but even as he spoke he realized just how hard it was going to be to control the words that came out of his mouth this evening.

'Yes, come on Michael, what'll you have? Can I get you an enormous amount of beer and a whoopee cushion?'

Sophie began to giggle uncontrollably but forced herself to stop when she saw that Jenny was not even smiling. Michael seemed quite unruffled, but there was a spark of amusement in his eyes that enraged Edward. Another anecdote to be passed on during his next encounter with a colleague in the toilets, no doubt: 'No word of a lie…that loony, Sewell, offered me – and I quote – "an enormous amount of beer and a whoopee cushion". A whoopee cushion, would you believe!'

A short silence ensued.

'Sorry,' apologized Edward, interpreting the message of his wife's raised eyebrow with what he confidently reckoned to be complete accuracy, 'just – just a joke. What'll you have?'

'Well, I think I'll pass on the whoopee cushion if it's all the same to you, Ted, but the enormous amount of beer sounds pretty good. One glass at a time'll do fine, though.'

'Well, the food's very nearly ready,' said Jenny, 'so get a beer for yourself as well, Edward, and bring them through to the dining-room. We'll start the wine a bit later. Come on you two, come and sit down.'

On his way from the kitchen to the dining-room with the beer, Edward met his wife on her way to collect the starters from the kitchen. He had feared he might. A hissed conversation was inevitable.

'Edward, what *is* the matter with you? What was all that about? Why are you in such a funny mood? Something's happened, hasn't it?'

'No.'

'Well, what has happened? Something's happened, whatever you say. I always know when something's happened. What is it?'

'Nothing. Nothing's happened. Well...'

'What?'

'Not so loud, they'll hear.'

'What, then?'

'No, honestly,' no, he wasn't going to tell her yet, 'I think it's just this headache, Jenny. I'm just a bit...you know.'

She moved her eyes close to his. 'No, I don't know, and I don't believe you. Go and sit down and look after them. Well, go on!'

At last they were all seated, each with their salad, chicken pâté and toast starter in front of them. Michael spread a little pâté on to a square of buttered toast, popped it into his mouth and chewed appreciatively.

'Mmm, delicious! Made with your own fair hands, Mrs Sewell?'

Jenny nodded and smiled.

'Which brings me to the third thing I was going to do just now,' went on Michael, busily spreading more butter and pâté as he spoke, 'and that was to say how much I'm looking forward to my mixed grill tonight. Wonderful idea! Why don't more hostesses dish it up at dinner parties?

I've been dreaming about it ever since the end of school today.'

'Mixed grill?'

Jenny's glass of wine, balanced between her first two fingers, hung suspended half-way to her lips as she stared at Michael.

'I think mixed grill's a reely good idea,' prattled Sophie happily. 'Blokes always like it 'cause there's a lot, and there's a nice variety if you don't like some sorts of meat, so you can...'

Her voice trailed off as she realized that something was not quite right.

'I'm sorry, Michael,' said Jenny, 'but what made you think we were having mixed grill tonight?'

Edward picked up one of the wine bottles and tilted it, licking his lips nervously as he watched the rich dark liquid fill his glass. Before he was able to think of anything to say, Michael was answering Jenny's question.

'What made me think...? Well, Edward told me, just before I left for home this afternoon. He said something about you not being sure you could get the chops or something, but it was definitely going to be mixed grill. Why? Isn't it? Any chance of a spot of wine for the rest of us, Ted?'

As Ted filled the glass in Michael's outstretched hand, he noted that his wife was slowly lowering her glass to the table and fixing him with a stare of utter incredulity. Swallowing hard, he adjusted his face to a setting that might approximate to some kind of normal reading.

'Edward?' Jenny's voice was a rich mixture of therapeutic calm, deep mystification and distant thunder.

'Mmm?' He had deliberately over-filled his mouth with pâté and toast in order to gain a little time.

'Edward, tell me – when you knew perfectly well that we were having seafood lasagne tonight, seeing as you suggested it and you bought most of the ingredients, why did you tell Michael that we were having a mixed grill?

Why on earth, Edward? Why? And what, in the name of the great Panjandrum is all this about me not being sure I could get chops? Why would I not be able to get chops?'

Everyone looked at Edward.

Edward, his eyes bulging, indicated his energetically working jaws and flapped his hands in apparent frustration, hoping to convincingly communicate the message: 'I have a truly excellent answer to that question on the tip of my tongue, and I cannot tell you how mortified I am by my inability to produce it at this precise moment owing to a large amount of food that I wish I had never placed in my mouth, but which simply has to be masticated before I even attempt to speak.'

'Well, seafood lasagne certainly suits us just as well,' smiled Michael lazily, 'a real treat, in fact. But I sure would like to know the solution to The Mystery of the Mixed Grill, by Agatha Sewell.'

Edward chewed and swallowed his way through his excuse at last and took a gulp of wine. Why, oh, why had he ever mentioned the *stupid* mixed grill? Why hadn't he kept his big mouth shut in the staffroom and just told Jenny what had happened when he got home, and let her sort it out? What a fool! What sort of ammunition was all this going to present Michael with in the weeks to come? So much for subtle revenge and the exercise of power! It was all going to end up the wrong way round. What on earth was he going to say now?

A brief reprieve came.

'I went on a seafood diet once,' said Sophie, who cherished a sweetly attractive and pathetically indomitable belief that the oldest and most well-worn of jokes would be unknown to her immediate circle. 'Every time I saw food I ate it.' She clapped a hand to her mouth and made little hissing noises like gas escaping. 'Oh, dear, I've messed that up, haven't I? I should have said I *am* on a seafood diet and every time I *see* food I *eat* it.' She looked disappointedly around the table. 'No wonder you all didn't laugh.'

There was a little polite tittering.

Edward tried to sound adult and assured. 'All right, the reason I told Michael we were having a mixed grill is very simple actually, Jenny, and the business about the chops is, if anything, even simpler. I got mixed up between two things. One was tonight's dinner and the other was – well, I can't tell you about it now because it's a surprise for…well, for a special occasion to do with you and me. I just got the two things crossed in my mind, that's all. I know it sounds mad, but there we are. Sorry, Michael. Sorry, Sophie.'

Sophie, who loved secrets, said, 'Oh, that's all right. Quite exciting, reely.'

Michael inclined his thinly covered head graciously, but that gleam of amusement was there in his eyes again. No doubt, thought Edward, it was all being stored up in readiness for a suitable occasion. As for Jenny – well, the bit about the special occasion had been something of an inspiration. There had always been an unspoken agreement between them that if some hint of a planned surprise was accidentally revealed by one to the other, then no more questions would be asked. He could tell that Jenny was far from convinced, and, sure as eggs, the reckoning would come, but at least he'd said *something*.

They ate for a while. No one spoke. Time to change the subject, thought Edward. The imp on his shoulder made an evil suggestion.

'Tell me, Michael, have you got to know any of the people in the maths department?'

'Why do you ask?'

'Oh, nothing really. I gather they've got real problems there. I wondered if you'd heard anything about it.'

'Well…' Michael swallowed his last piece of toast and wiped his mouth with his napkin, 'as far as I can see there's only one major problem and that's the man in charge.'

'Oh, dear, same old problem. Do I know him, Edward?' asked Jenny. 'Plates, please.'

'Name of Salmons,' said Michael, passing his plate and almost turning himself inside-out with a wide yawn. 'Oh, dear, sorry – nothing to do with the company I assure you. Just a little tired.'

Turned out a bit of a wake, has it, Michael?

'No, he's a funny bloke in some ways. Older man. Retires next year. Bit dry and cynical. Never hit it off with his own staff at all. That's the main problem, I should imagine. I don't know him all that well, but we've had the occasional chat over the years. As far as I can recall he's never had a good word to say for anyone. I tell you, the milk of human kindness hasn't just dried up in that bloke – it's curdled.'

'Poor man,' observed Jenny with compassion, as she picked up the plates that the starters had been on and turned to leave the room, 'it must be horrible to end up like that.'

'I'll come and give you a hand with everything,' squeaked Sophie, pushing her chair back, 'I don't want to hear any more about a sad man with a name like some fish. I was useless at maths.'

Edward felt quite scared when he was left alone with Michael. There were so many different strata in this precipice of a situation that he hardly knew who either of them really were. He felt guilty about not telling Jenny, and he still felt angry, and he felt stupid because he was bound to end up feeling worse than Michael. Stupid, stupid, stupid!

'I tell a lie,' said Michael, leaning forward with his elbow on the table and raising a finger, 'old Salmons did say something nice about someone, and I should have remembered, because it was only today he came out with it. I meant to tell you what he said only it went out of my head until just this moment.'

'Is this the serious talk you said you wanted to have with me?'

'What?' Michael's sauvity deserted him for about half a second. 'Oh, no, no, that's something else. We'll do that later. No, this was something Salmons said about you.'

'About me?'

'That's right – now let me just think of the exact words.' He held his thumb and second finger level with his face and slightly apart for an instant then brought them together, snapping his fingers, then shaking a fore-finger in triumph. 'That's it! I'd just been saying that you and I have been friends since we first came, and then I said I was coming to dinner with you tonight and he said: "Best English teacher this school's ever had." Those were his exact words. "Best English teacher this school's ever had." What d'you think of that, then? Quite a compliment coming from a dry old stick like that, eh?'

'Mmm, yes, indeed!' replied Edward, somewhat heavily role-playing surprise and pleasure. 'Yes, that is quite a compliment. Beats me how he would come to that conclusion, mind you. He's never seen me teach that I'm aware of.'

'Well, there's exam results for a start. Speak for themselves, don't they? And these things get around – through the kids, other members of staff, it's a funny little gossipy village, a school, isn't it, Ted?'

Yes, Michael, a funny little gossipy village.

'But how did this come about, then, Michael – you and friend Salmons chatting about me, I mean? Seems a bit unlikely somehow. Have some…?'

He offered the wine once more to Michael, who held out his glass and nodded thanks. For the first time that evening Edward was beginning to enjoy himself. Michael took a sip from his glass and shrugged.

'Oh, we just ran into each other at the end of school and got chatting. I think he asked me what I was doing tonight, and, like I said, I told him that Sophie and I had the very good fortune to be coming to supper in Oxford Avenue with two of my favourite people, and that's when he said that about your teaching. Can't be all bad, can he?'

'Still, I am surprised,' said Edward reflectively. 'I sometimes get the impression that an awful lot of the staff see me as a sort of in-house loony. Do you know what I mean?'

For a moment he thought he might have gone too far. For one tiny fraction of a second Michael seemed to twitch inwardly, as if an unexpected connection had been made, then the moment was past, and, seeing in Michael's face an expression of sternly serious intent, Edward realized with a sense of wonder and horror, that he was about to be encouraged!

'Edward Sewell,' Michael raised his right hand flat in the air, pointing into Edward's face with the tips of his fingers, 'don't you ever let me hear you run yourself down like that again. I don't know if anyone does think stupid things like that, but I can tell you one thing. They'd better not try passing their views on to me, whoever they are. They'll get more than they've bargained for.' He gave a little self-deprecatory laugh. 'In any case, if you're a – what was it?'

'A loony, Michael.'

'If you're a loony, and I'm your friend, what does that make me?'

Well, basically that makes you a lying, treacherous, son of a...

'So no more of that, thank you, Mr Sewell. By the way,' Michael glanced at the door before leaning across the table to speak in conspiratorially hushed tones, 'what's this mystery event that won't work unless mixed grill's on the menu? You want to watch it, mate, you nearly let the cat out of the bag there, didn't you? What's going on? Anniversary or something?'

Suddenly Edward was no longer enjoying himself. Oh, what a tangled web...

'Shush, they're coming back.'

The meal continued in a sort of fog as far as Edward was concerned. Michael repeated Salmons' comment for Jenny's sake (Jenny was really pleased, as he'd known she would be), and he also repeated the gist of that little stern lecture he had delivered, offering to Jenny his considered view that Edward should give himself greater credit for his achievements and be more prepared to trust that his friends would always support him in the event of criticism. Jenny heartily agreed – so did Sophie. Edward nearly brought up his seafood lasagne.

It was at this point that Edward fought, and succeeded in overcoming, a strong temptation to regale the company with an anecdote about his last visit to the hairdresser's, when the girl who always did his trim had complimented him on having such a luxuriant head of hair. She had also expressed a particular interest in, and admiration for, the fact that his hair showed not a trace of grey, despite what obviously seemed to her his relatively advanced age. He fantasized about following this account with merciless repetition of its salient points. 'Luxuriant, this girl said, Michael, meaning a great deal of it, you understand. More than I need. Enough for two. Lots of it. Lots and lots of hair. Lots of thick, dark, luxuriant hair with no grey in it, the sort of hair that pathetic sub-male baldies like you would love to have but can't because they're getting bald, bald, bald!'

He could taste the words, hot on his tongue, but the very thought of losing control and actually saying such dreadful, childish things in front of his wife and the trust-ing Sophie made him shiver inside. The sooner this farce of a meal ended the better. He knew that there was bound to be instant interrogation as soon as the front door had closed behind their two guests, but at least he would be free to say exactly what he thought then, and Jenny could surely not fail to be sympathetic when she knew what had happened. In the meantime, perhaps assuming that her husband was suffering from some kind of brainstorm, she had obviously decided to take charge of the situation, and, as usual, she really did do a very good job, encouraging Michael and Sophie to talk at length about themselves and their future plans. A topic of conversation, reflected Edward, that never ceases to provide hours of fascination for those who are doing the talking.

It was over coffee that Michael, who had spent some time outlining the future of P.E. teaching as he envisioned it, leaned back in his chair and said, 'What about the old poetry, Ted? These evenings of ours wouldn't be complete without an offering from the bard of Oxford Avenue, would they, Sofe?'

Sophie, who had never managed to understand a single line of Edward's poetry, smiled and nodded good-humouredly, looking forward to the time, hopefully not far in the future now, when she and Jenny would disappear into the kitchen to wash up and gossip while the two husbands drank their brandy in the dining-room.

Edward thought he had made a firm decision not to react negatively to anything else that the other man might say in the course of the evening, but this comment simply took his breath away. Why was Michael actually *asking* to hear some of the 'entrails' that he despised and found so boring? He pulled himself together. This time he was prepared.

'Could you pass that notebook, darling, please, just there on the side. Yes, that's the one. Thanks.' He flicked through the pages until he came to the one he wanted. 'There was something I thought you might like to hear actually,' he said. 'It's more doggerel than poetry, and it's not really finished, not honed, if you know what I mean, but…well, you see what you think.'

Sensitivity makes you very sensitive, thought Edward, glancing up in time to register an almost imperceptible tilt of Michael's wrist, as the younger man contemplated a glance at his watch, then thought better of it.

Jenny was looking a little puzzled. Usually, she was asked to read and comment on Edward's new work before anyone else was allowed so much as to sniff at it.

Sophie frowned and leaned foward. She looked as if she was straining to locate those hitherto undiscovered muscles which, when flexed, might aid comprehension.

'Fire away,' said Michael, 'looking forward to this.'

'Right, well, "United In Glory" is the title,' announced Edward. He began to read from his notebook:

'Duncan Edwards, once the best,
Went early to his well-earned rest,
To find God nursed a secret dream,
Of managing a football team,
Seeing Munich made God sad,
But keen to rescue good from bad,
Couldn't help but be delighted,
Most of Manchester United,
Turned up at the Pearly Gates,
Good old Duncan with his mates,
They were offered free salvation,
Pending full negotiation,
Contracts stating that the fee,
Would bind them for eternity,
(Transfer bans were just as well,
The only place to go was hell)
Wages well worth playing for,
The love of God for ever more,
Practised kicks and moves and passes,
Over heaven's shining grasses,
None more expert than their boss,
(A long-time expert on the cross)
He laid on boots and kit and towels,
But vetoed all professional fouls,
Aware the team was not complete,
He said he'd need to slightly cheat,
So, doing the pragmatic thing,

He put an angel on the wing.
At last, God's team lined up with pride,
To play Old Nick's infernal side,
And watched by several billion souls,
Heaven won by thirteen goals,
Duncan, who'd put seven in,
Asked God what made him sure they'd win,
Said God, 'No miracles required,
You did it all, a team inspired,
Besides, I knew that, as a rule,
Hell recruits from Liverpool.'

It was one of *the* most gratifying moments that Edward had known for a very long time. All three of the others sitting round the table had been visibly jerked out of their common perception of him by the words he had just read. Michael, for instance, looked, to use an example of modern slang that Edward had tended to abhor in the classroom but particularly relished in private, veritably gobsmacked. Jenny, leaning back in her chair with folded arms, was gazing at her husband with a rare combination of shock, wariness and concern, rather as if she was beginning to suspect that he might be an imposter – an Edward Sewell dopplegänger. Sophie was surprised but delighted. She had heard all about the Munich air disaster from her husband. For once, she felt that she had understood quite a lot of one of Edward's poems. She was the first to make a comment.

'Oh, Eddie, that was reely good, I mean it. The way you made it all – you know. That was reely good, wasn't it, Mike? All about your team too. Reely good!'

'It was excellent,' agreed Mike, looking rather puzzled, but sounding more connected than he had all evening. 'I'd really like a copy of that, Ted, if you don't mind. Completely different from your usual stuff. I didn't know you were a United fan.'

So satisfying, thought Edward, to look into Michael's eyes and see a sudden shift in the foundations of his infuriatingly confident assumption that he knew exactly what to expect from E. Sewell, the old idiot whom, he had very kindly said, he wouldn't want to actually upset.

'Oh, I'm not a United fan,' he replied, 'I was just fiddling around earlier and came up with that. It's nothing really.'

There was a short silence.

'Right!' Jenny smacked the table lightly with the palms of her hands. 'I think it's about time you and I attacked the Baileys, don't you, Sophie? Let's leave these two...' throwing a sardonic glance in Edward's direction 'football fanatics to chew the turf together while we get things a bit cleared up in the kitchen.'

'Ooh, yes,' responded Sophie enthusiastically, 'there's something I wanted to ask you about.'

Oh, dear, thought Edward, as the two women left the room, everyone seems to have something to say to someone else. Michael was presumably about to mention the 'something serious' that was on his mind, Sophie wanted to ask Jenny about something, Jenny would undoubtedly be planning to grill Edward intensively just as soon as their guests had gone, and he, himself – did he have anything further to say to this man who appeared to despise him in reality, but continually offered shallow blandishments to his face? Perhaps.

'Ted, I wonder if we could have a little chat?'

It was a few minutes later. An opened brandy bottle stood on the table between them, and a good measure of the precious liquid had been poured into two of the extravagantly bulbous glasses, inherited from his father, that Edward loved to hold and look at and drink from.

'Have we come to the serious bit now, then, Michael?' Edward held his glass in front of his eyes and studied its contents with deep concentration. Perhaps the secret of life itself would be revealed if he were to peer into that twinkling amber world for long enough.

'It's about these evenings of ours,' said Michael, the pitch of his voice very slightly higher than usual. 'There's something – I wondered if we could just talk about one thing that's been part of us getting together like this. Don't get me wrong. As I said earlier, I really relax when I come here, and Sophie gets on like a house on fire with Jenny, so it's not, you know, anything big. It's just that almost every time we have dinner together, round about now, when the girls are out of the way, we – you have sort of been in the habit of bringing up the past. All the stuff about church background and that kind of thing. We do talk about that almost every time we have dinner together, don't we?'

'You'd rather we didn't talk about it at all?' Edward continued to stare into the depths of his glass.

Michael sucked air in through his teeth and rubbed the top of his head vigorously with the tips of his fingers to indicate the intensity of his wish to avoid giving offence. Careful, Michael, thought Edward, you'll rub the fluff away.

'Look, Ed, that poem of yours just now – really good. Like I said, you must let me have a copy – that poem says what you and I really think about religion. It's a game. It's a picture of what a lot of people wish was true. But that's all it is. My mother and father totally believed every word of it because they were fully-committed, born-again types, and even your dad was well into it, wasn't he, although perhaps not in the same way that they were. When I was small I just got caught up and brainwashed like you can easily do when you're a kid, but, well, it was a long time ago, Ed, and – I have to be quite honest with you – I really would prefer to put it all behind me now and just leave it there. Our parents were good people, but – but they were deluded. That's the bottom line for me. I just want to ask if we can leave it off the old agenda from now on because I feel as if I'm being dragged backwards every time we talk about it. What do you say?'

Everything inside Edward had suddenly become very still. He did indeed feel as if an important secret might have been communicated to him, but not from the depths of the brandy. He lowered his glass a little and looked straight into the other man's eyes. When he spoke, his voice was quiet and controlled.

'What did you mean when you said "*even* your dad was well into it"?' Michael frowned and shook his head, somewhat nonplussed. 'I just meant that he was a traditional Anglican as opposed to a spirit-filled believer, that's all. What difference does it make?'

'And what exactly is the difference between a spirit-filled believer and a traditional Anglican?'

'Well, basically, Christians like the ones in my parents' church are aware that the Holy Spirit is just as important a member of the Trinity as the Father and the Son, and they've been baptized in the Spirit as well as by water, which is what Jesus said had to happen, and they use all the gifts of the Spirit, like prophecy and tongues and healing, all the things that Paul talks about so much in the New Testament. They're true, born-again children of God.'

'Who doesn't exist.'

'Err, that's right.'

'And traditional Anglicans?'

Michael swirled the brandy around in the bottom of his glass and took a tiny sip. 'Well, the general view in our church was that what you might call the mainline denominations, Anglicans, Methodists and so on, were in serious danger of missing the boat, or, to use a different metaphor that our pastor once suggested in one of his talks, they're dead limbs on the Christian tree, and will need to be lopped off in the end.'

'My father was a dry twig on a dead limb?' Edward's voice was still very quiet.

'Well, only if you believe in it all. Look...' Michael moved the brandy bottle and a salt cellar like chess pieces as he assembled his ideas, 'you don't have to believe it all to see the sense of it, surely. Much earlier this century God looks around the country and he sees a load of highly respectable, middle-class people trooping along to church every Sunday, purely out of habit, with no real idea of why they're going, and he says to himself, "Right, I've had enough of this. I'm going to set up churches full of believers who are genuinely committed, and anyone from the traditional denominations who wants can leave the church they're in and join one of the new ones. I'll leave spiritual gravity to finish off the old, lifeless ones. They'll just drop off when they're completely dead, or if not, I'll give 'em a little push." '

'So, in your opinion, my father was not a true believer.'

'Well, I didn't know him, Ted, so it's impossible for me to judge. He may have been an exception to the rule, for all I know. But as we know it's all nonsense anyway, what does it matter?'

Edward felt the suspicion of tears pricking the back of his eyelids. 'He prayed every single morning of his life after I was born that I would become a Christian. That's not bad for a dead twig, is it?' Michael just shrugged. 'And your mum and dad, Michael – you're saying, aren't you, that they were totally, one hundred per cent deluded? You are saying that, aren't you? You're saying that the thing they gave their whole life to was nothing but a game. A picture, I think you called it, didn't you?' He waited. 'Well?'

It was a strange moment. Michael's mouth was certainly moving and attempting to frame words, as though there was something he wanted to say in reply, but it was in his eyes that Edward read an admission and a silent pleading, a request for permission to be at peace in this matter. Could it be possible that they had experienced the same revelation this evening? For Edward was reeling inwardly from the shock of knowing something now that he had never known before, although the truth of it was a part of him. Perhaps it always had been. Michael's absurd distinctions had provided the final clarification. His father had not been deluded, or rather, he was not a man in whom such a delusion could find a lifetime's home. Of course he wasn't! The spirit of his father, as real to Edward today as when that dear man had been alive, that warm amalgam of gentleness, kindness, generosity and faith could never have been dependent for sustenance on a picture or a game. There was no delusion, except in the subtle denial of his own true responses. What Edward was experiencing was not a conversion, but a restoration of clear sight. And those who can see are more easily able to choose which path to take.

Michael's eyes had lost the battle with his mouth. 'It was a good enough game as games go,' said the mouth, 'but that's all it was, and I don't want to think about it any more if it's all the same to you, Ted.'

'Okay, Michael, I promise I won't mention it again unless you do. All right?'

'Fine – thanks,' said the mouth. Hold on to me, said the eyes.

Edward took a risk. 'There's one condition, though.'

'A condition?'

'Yes.' Edward tore a clean sheet of paper from the pad which was still lying on the table, and passed it across. 'I want you to write the truth on this piece of paper, then fold it up and give it to me to keep.'

'The truth?'

Michael's very visible attempt to pretend that he had not the faintest idea what Edward was talking about failed almost immediately. The sardonic smile simply would not be resurrected. For a second or two he stared at the blank sheet of paper in his hands, then, laying it down on the table, he took a slimly elegant Biro from the inside pocket of his jacket, clicked it, and wrote busily for about a minute. Finally, after stabbing the paper with a final fullstop, he put his pen away, folded the sheet neatly three times, and handed it back to Edward.

'I have a feeling we must have both gone stark staring bonkers,' he said with weary resignation, 'but there you are – take it. You can read it if you want, but only after I've gone. And we don't talk about it any more, right?'

'Right,' agreed Edward, 'I promise,' and he poured a little more brandy into both their glasses.

Half an hour later, when the usual twittering goodbyes and assurances of reunion had been completed, and the front door had finally closed behind Michael and Sophie, Edward put his arms around his wife in the hall. She stayed there for a few moments before drawing back and studying his face at arm's length.

'What happened today, Edward? If you say "nothing" I shall get a large, flat kitchen implement and beat you with it.'

'Promises, promises!' Edward smiled, feeling very tired suddenly. 'I was in the toilets at school today and I overheard Michael talking to that bloke Salmons about me and you and tonight's dinner party.'

Jenny gasped. 'What did he say?'

Edward repeated the conversation as accurately as memory would allow. 'He was nice about you,' he said in conclusion, 'said he'd got a lot of time for you, Mrs Loony.'

'Oh, Edward, darling, what a little rat. You must have been so upset. Why on earth didn't you tell me when you got back?'

He thought for a moment. 'Mmm, lots of bad reasons. I suppose I should have done really, shouldn't I? But, in fact, as it's turned out…' He laughed. 'You never did believe in my silly headache, did you? What did Sophie want to ask you, by the way?'

'Oh, yes, she said that she and Michael were wondering if we would be willing to do one of those things for little Paul where we agree to take him in and bring him up if his mum and dad get killed in a car crash or something.

But after hearing about your toilet experience I can't understand why. Why us? Why Mr and Mrs Loony?'

'As far as Sophie's concerned it's obvious. She thinks the sun shines out of your back door…'

'Edward!'

'So who could possibly make a better substitute mum for Paul if anything happened to her? And she's right. I agree with her. As for Michael…' he shook his head slowly from side to side, 'well, much more complicated, I think. Jenny, something happened this evening that we need to talk about. Not now, I don't mean, but soon – I haven't really sorted it out for myself yet. Tomorrow, perhaps.'

She yawned. 'Tomorrow will do. Do you think you'll ever tell Michael you heard all those things he said?'

Edward thought for a moment then shook his head. 'Too late – should have told him today if I was going to. No, I shan't.'

'Let's go to bed, Edward. Nothing matters much till the morning, and it's blessed, wonderful Saturday tomorrow, so we can sleep in if we want.'

Edward and Jenny were both asleep by eleven thirty. At three o'clock in the morning the extension telephone in their bedroom rang. Edward always said that when the phone rang at that time of night it could only be bad news or an Australian. Jenny answered it. This time it was bad news. Michael had suffered some kind of massive heart attack during the night, and had been rushed by ambulance to the hospital where Jenny did her part-time job, the nearest with an accident and emergency unit. It was the hospital on the phone now, passing on a message to say that Paul was safely with a neighbour, but Sophie had asked if Jenny could come and be with her at Casualty.

'Oh, poor, poor Sophie!' said Jenny, with tears in her eyes, as she struggled into her clothes, 'she'll be like a little wet handkerchief.' She put a hand over her mouth. 'Oh, Edward, I called him a rat last night. I wish I hadn't. You will come with me, won't you?'

The cold, dead weight of shock kept them both silent as they drove down the virtually deserted main road to the hospital. All that Edward could think of was Sophie's open, pretty face crumpled with grief, and Michael's worry over his thin hair. Thinking of the hair especially kept making him want to cry. They arrived at the hospital just before half-past three.

Michael died at six thirty that same morning, having failed to regain consciousness sufficiently to communicate with anyone. The next few hours were all about Jenny looking after Sophie, who alternated between silent, blank puzzlement and floods of tears throughout the morning. In the early afternoon she fell into a troubled sleep on the sitting-room sofa, exhausted by grief and lack of sleep. Jenny and Edward, worn out themselves, sat over strong coffee in the kitchen, letting whatever was in their heads come out in words.

'At least, wherever Michael is,' said Jenny, after a while, 'he knows his little boy is safe.'

Edward nodded agreement, but at Jenny's words an abstracted look came into his eyes. He pushed his chair back and stood up.

'Look, I think I'll go for a bit of a stroll,' he announced, 'just round the block – get some air. You can go when I get back if you want.'

It was a bright, frosty day, sparkling but cold. From the end of Oxford Avenue, Edward took the short cut through to the main road, turned right and walked briskly past the High Street shops until he arrived at the bottom of a flight of stone steps leading up to the austere frontage of St John's, the parish church where his father had been a regular worshipper for many years. Climbing the steps, he hesitated for a moment, then turned the handle of the big front door and pushed hard. To his slight surprise, it was unlocked. Slipping quickly into the church he leaned back against the door, clicking it shut behind him.

Inside, the hushed silence was almost a shock, the temperature even lower than it had been in the open air. Shivering with cold and vague apprehension, he made himself walk purposefully up the wide central aisle between row after row of long, dark-stained Victorian pews towards the east end of the church. Ascending two shallow steps to the cloth-covered altar, he stopped and rubbed his chilled hands together for a moment. Before him, one at each end of the altar, stood two majestically large brass candlesticks.

'I could steal those if I wanted to,' he murmured quietly to himself, 'but I don't think I will.'

Undoing two top overcoat buttons he reached inside his jacket pocket with numbed fingers, to locate and draw out the folded piece of paper that Michael had left with him the night before. Carefully unfolding it, he studied the words that had been written with close attention, nodding gently, as if not at all surprised by what he read. Refolding the sheet, he closed his eyes, and held it up in front of him in both hands for a few seconds, before laying it gently down on the flat surface of the altar.

After backing slowly down the steps, Edward sat huddled on the front pew for a little while. One stumbling prayer for Michael and Sophie, and one for himself and Jenny, then, suddenly embarrassed, he hurried out of the church into the brittle winter sunshine and the ice-cream air.

Stanley Morgan's Minor Misdemeanour

It was the woman's eyes that changed everything. She had such beautiful eyes, warm and liquid, with a greenish tinge. He wanted to dive into them in slow motion, just slide quietly into their depths and swim lazily around. Every now and then he dreamed that he was doing exactly that. Sometimes his dreams had nothing to do with swimming. He doubted that those dreams would ever come true, because, if they did, it would mean that he had committed a sin, and Stanley Morgan had never been very good at sin.

Even before becoming a Christian in his early twenties, Stanley's life had been a strikingly mild affair. Fear of the wild, unknown country that must surely await those who strayed from the path of rectitude had always been stronger than the occasional desire to step out and explore things that his mother and father had taught him to regard as unequivocally wrong.

Only once, just after his sixteenth birthday, had he attempted a wholehearted submission to temptation, and even that had gone ridiculously awry.

Transported by lust and the local bus service, Stanley had travelled to a market town several miles away from the one where he lived, with the sole intention of buying and secretly reading a copy of *Penthouse Magazine*. At the end of the bumpy half-hour journey this desire to feast his eyes on photographs of naked female flesh was still burning just sufficiently to propel him into the newsagent's shop next to the railway station, but it was a struggle from that point onwards. He spent a ludicrous amount of time gazing earnestly at items of stationery, racks of greetings cards and boxes of chocolates.

Eventually, face flaming, he laid a pad of writing paper, two Biros, one Mars Bar, a copy of the *Daily Telegraph* and *the* magazine down on the counter at the far end of the shop. He clutched at a pathetically optimistic hope that the attractive, modestly dressed young lady who was about to take his money would say to herself, 'Ah, here we have the sort of respectable person who reads the *Daily Telegraph*. He's probably going to use this pad and these Biros to do some kind of objective research on the contents of this vile magazine that he couldn't possibly have bought for any other purpose.'

Certainly, the girl did throw a curious glance at the youth with the beetroot-red face, and eyes that would not meet hers, but it was only much later in life that Stanley was able to reflect ruefully on the fact that she probably connected such palpable embarrassment with his choice of newspaper, rather than his purchase of the magazine.

Escaping from the shop, Stanley swallowed hard, mopped his brow, rolled his *Penthouse* up in his *Telegraph*, and stepped out in a manner which he hoped might be construed as non-lustful purposefulness by anyone who might care to watch him, away from the shops and houses, up the tree-lined hill behind the coach station, and along a narrow footpath that curled its way across the bracken-covered common behind the town. After following the path for two or three hundred yards, he glanced swiftly around, then changed direction abruptly, walking straight into the middle of the waist-high green fronds, and ducking out of sight with an abruptness that would have surprised and alarmed anyone who happened to witness his dramatically sudden descent.

Down in the unexpectedly cosy, green-lit chamber, shaped and formed by the weight of his own body, Stanley shivered deliciously with sheer pleasure at the thought of the warm wickedness to come.

Now!

Extracting the Mars Bar from his jacket pocket, he peeled its wrapper back and bit half an inch off one end, then, shifting to a more comfortable position, he unrolled his paper, feverishly anticipating a feast of photographs displaying all the female curves and crevices he had so often imagined but never actually seen in real life.

The magazine was not there.

No matter how much he shook his newspaper and pulled its pages apart, that magazine, the focus of his one excursion into deliberate, organized evil, just wasn't there. He must have dropped it somewhere between the shop and the point where he'd turned off the path. It must have just slid out and fallen to the ground without him noticing as he walked along. Were there to be no female curves and crevices? No nothing? Oh – rats!

Stanley's self-image, far from buoyant at the best of times, sank to an even lower level. Here he was, after much careful plotting and planning, concealed among thick bracken in a deserted place, with nothing more lascivious than a partly eaten Mars Bar and the *Daily Telegraph*. What a fool! About to stand up, he paused, wondering what passers-by would think if they spotted him rising from the undergrowth with a newspaper clutched in his hand. They'd think – goodness knows what they'd think!

When he did finally get to his feet, there was only one person in sight. An elderly, barrel-shaped, waddling little man, closely accompanied by an elderly, barrel-shaped, waddling little dog, seemed so deeply engrossed in some kind of reading matter as he strolled slowly along that he noticed neither Stanley's tentative ascent to the outside world, nor his breathless, panic-stricken series of hopping strides to the implied respectability of the footpath.

So relieved was Stanley to escape unobserved from his hiding place that it wasn't until a minute or so after passing the stroller and his dog that he realized what the absorbing reading matter in the man's hands must be. He had caught the merest glimpse of something flesh-coloured and pneumatic without registering what it was. It was – surely it had to be – his missing magazine. Stopping dead on the path and turning on his heel, Stanley tried to picture himself catching the man up and demanding the return of his *Penthouse*, but his nerve failed him. He couldn't do it. He simply could not face the idea of laying claim to that garish symbol of wrongdoing.

The bus journey home was not a happy one. Every bump was a penance.

The rest of the Mars Bar turned to ashes in his mouth. The *Telegraph* was boring.

Years passed, but the memory of that day haunted Stanley. It had been the one occasion in his life when he had committed (or attempted to commit) a carefully considered act of rebellion. He regretted it for four reasons. Three of these he was able to admit to himself, and one he wasn't.

First, he felt guilty about doing it at all. The very thought of his neat, confident, morally organized mother or his small, broad, fiercely trouser-braced father finding out what he had tried to do, sent a shiver of horror right through his body.

Secondly, he felt guilty about the barrel-shaped, waddling man who had found his magazine on the path that day. Suppose, he asked himself worriedly, that man had been a nice, clean, uncorrupted sort of person before encountering the sea of curves and crevices that were undoubtedly depicted on the pages that he had been studying with such concentration? Might Stanley have been inadvertently but nevertheless culpably responsible for an innocent man's moral downfall?

Thirdly, he was deeply troubled by the revelation of potential evil within himself. If it had been possible for temptation to lead him from the narrow path (literally and figuratively) for that short distance on that one occasion, was it not likely that, down on some dark and desperate level of his personality, there lurked hidden impulses to attempt even more extravagant excursions, or perhaps even to abandon the path altogether? Stanley decided to work hard at developing the habit of keeping tight reins on his thoughts and feelings in order to obviate such an unwelcome possibility.

The fourth regret, one that Stanley found it quite impossible to look at clearly, was actually a species of mourning for something quite indefinable that he might, or perhaps even should, have discovered, but didn't, on the common that day. In a misty, confused sort of way he remembered the short, unsatisfactory space of time in which he had been buried in his Stanley-shaped, dark green, brackeny world, as an encounter with a woman, someone soft and sweet who had dissolved in his arms at the moment when that unrolled newspaper had revealed his loss. There were times, in unguarded moments, when this strange and powerful non-memory would invade his peace so forcefully that he felt like crying, but the experience always confused and disoriented him. How could something so cheap and sordid and downright silly from the past produce feelings of such sad beauty in the present? The answer was, of course, that it couldn't. Stanley pushed these feelings back down into himself whenever they appeared, but on a deeper level still, he yearned to meet that 'woman' again.

Becoming a Christian at the age of twenty-three felt to Stanley like a solution to his most pressing problems. The recent death of his parents, within less than six months of each other, had naturally distressed him greatly, but it had also left him with a little knot of panic in his chest that seemed to never quite become untied. Silly questions flashed into his mind and had to be dismissed because they didn't make any sense.

Who would be his mother and father now?

Who was sure enough about what you do and what you don't do to keep him on the right track?

Getting involved with a fellowship that met on Sunday mornings at one of the local junior schools not far from his home was exactly what he needed. The person in charge was very strong and supportive, and most of the people who went were enthusiastic and easy to get along with. Everyone seemed to want to be clean, and free from sin, just as Stanley did. Being part of such a body gave him a good, safe feeling, especially after he joined the house-group that gathered just before eight o'clock every Wednesday evening at Brian and Madge Ford's house. Brian and Madge were the leaders of the group. They took a close, pastoral interest in each fellowship member entrusted to them by the eldership of the church, and their attitude to Stanley was no exception. Both of them were very warm and caring indeed towards him and he liked and respected them greatly.

On the occasion of his fifth attendance at the Wednesday meeting, Stanley made an announcement to the other group members as everybody sat, as usual, around the edge of the Fords' conveniently large sitting-room, on bean-bags, dining-room chairs and a big comfortable three-piece suite, drinking coffee, tea or squash after the Bible-study and time of prayer. He had reached a decision about his life in general and his spiritual life in particular, he told them. He wanted to make a personal commitment to Christ. There was much rejoicing as a result. In fact, he could not have hoped for a more gratifying response. It turned out that Stanley's conversion was the answer to a great deal of prayer on the part of just about everyone present. After Brian had helped him to say his own prayer of commitment, and several other folk had thanked God for working so effectively in Stanley's heart, Madge disappeared into the kitchen, returning a few moments later with a newly-opened bottle of wine and some glasses so that the house-group could celebrate the beginning of their new brother's walk with the Lord.

It was the first time that Stanley had relaxed inside for a very long while. He could almost feel that knot in his chest untying itself – or perhaps he should say – *being* untied. It was such a relief.

There was one worry. Stanley wanted everything in his new life to be as right and as clean as it could possibly be. He arranged to see Brian privately, indicating that there was something serious in his past that needed to be dealt with and forgiven. When the two men met, Brian quietly assured Stanley that there was no sin so terrible that it could not be confessed to God and forgiven by the power of the resurrection of Christ. They faced each other in silence across Brian's kitchen table for at least two minutes after that, but finally Stanley summoned up the courage to describe what had happened on the common all those years ago. It was a hard thing to do, but the feeling of relief afterwards was so wonderful that he found himself shedding a tear or two.

At first, Brian had seemed just a little taken aback by the exact nature of Stanley's 'serious' sin, but, clearly sensing how important the memory was to the nervous young man sitting at the other side of the table, he had responded with entirely appropriate gravity, quietly asking one or two relevant questions and nodding solemnly at the answers.

Encouraged by his house-group leader, who was a firm believer in practical spirituality, Stanley prayed out loud for forgiveness, and thanked God that the magazine, the vehicle of temptation, had slipped from his grasp during that walk across the common. They both prayed for the barrel-shaped waddling man, asking that he also should be forgiven for any sin arising from his exposure to those potentially corrupting images, and pleading that, if he was still alive, he should find Jesus for himself and inherit the eternal life promised to all those who are hidden in Christ.

Finally, Stanley asked if it would be all right to make an apology to his parents posthumously, as it were. Brian carefully explained that the Bible tends to frown on actual attempts to communicate with the dead, but went on to say that, in his opinion, it would be perfectly all right for Stanley to tell God how much he regretted doing something that would have hurt his mother and father if they'd known about it. That would be almost the same as apologizing directly to them, he suggested. It was.

All in all, it was a most satisfactory experience for Stanley. He was not metaphorically inclined, generally speaking, but he told Brian that it was as if he had just pulled out some heavy piece of furniture that hadn't been shifted for years, and finally faced the task of cleaning away the muck that had been allowed to accumulate behind it. Brian congratulated him on the aptness of the metaphor, and gently pointed out that light cleaning on a daily basis would mean that he'd probably never need to move any heavy pieces of furniture again. Stanley liked this idea very much, and made it the basis of his prayer life from that day onwards. Whenever daily devotions were discussed in the house-group, Stanley's contribution was always the same. A little light dusting, he would tell them – that was what he did every morning – a little light dusting. Then he would smile at Brian, and Brian would smile back. It was something special between them. It gave Stanley a warm, secure feeling. He belonged, and his feet were safely on the path. No more excursions for him.

More years passed, and that other memory, the one that wasn't really a memory, the one that quite erroneously placed an aura of sweetness and loss around an event that was actually an experience of sin and temptation, was buried so deeply inside Stanley, that, if he had been asked, and if he had understood the question, he would have replied that it had gone altogether. He had never mentioned those strange, meaningless yearnings to Brian, partly because he would have been unable to put them into words, but mainly because it was the only genuine pearl he had, and, although he didn't know it, giving it away would have left little or no reason for hanging on to the field in which it was hidden.

Very occasionally, a shadow did pass unexpectedly across the bright regularity of his life, but Stanley was gradually aquiring techniques for dealing with such problems. One Sunday, for instance, a visiting speaker at the fellowship had instructed everybody in what to do when the devil knocked at the door of their lives, trying to peddle his deception and lies.

Send Jesus to answer the door – that was his recommendation.

Stanley found this piece of advice particularly helpful, and employed the speaker's suggestion whenever his equilibrium was threatened by seductive shadows or temptation or inappropriate stimulation. He became very good at it. In fact, so much of a habit did it become to send Jesus to the door that he more or less abandoned the idea of ever answering it himself. Why take the risk?

Life was peaceful and good.

From the time of his conversion, Stanley had prayed consistently, if not passionately, that he might one day be married and have children of his own. Having a family, he felt, would see him comfortably through to that important point where he would need to take just the one necessary stride from the end of his earthly path on to the streets of heaven. The girl – or woman, he should say nowadays, of course – would have to be a Christian, naturally, that went without saying, and he was a little troubled about how the sex thing would work itself out – you couldn't have a family without that happening. If they were both Christians, though, he told himself, there would be few problems that could not be solved through prayer and patience.

He was absolutely right. Three days after his twenty-seventh birthday a new person called Alison joined the house-group (still run by Brian and Madge, though some of the old members had left and been replaced by others), and from the moment Stanley saw her he somehow knew that this newcomer was one day to be his wife. Later, after they had become engaged, Alison told Stanley that she had felt exactly the same when she first saw him. They treasured the knowledge of this coincidence that, of course, wasn't a coincidence at all, welcoming it as confirmation of the rightness of their plans to be united as man and wife.

The avoidance of sex before getting married was more of a problem for Alison than Stanley, but she also enjoyed the fact that he was being so strongly principled in that area. Stanley rather enjoyed the feeling that he was being strongly principled as well, and actually did almost believe that he was.

The wedding itself was a marvellous occasion. Most of the fellowship turned up to witness the ceremony, and Stanley invited one or two colleagues from the Land Registry in Cambridge where he worked, not just because they were friends, but also because it was a good opportunity for them to hear the Gospel in an indirect but nevertheless very effective way. They could hardly have failed to be impressed. The singing was loud and enthusiastic, and the fellowship leader's talk was wise but humorous. Alison's widowed mother, who had found Stanley highly satisfactory from the moment she first met him, later described the service as 'deeply moving'.

The reception was a bright, happy occasion. It made Stanley feel very special and important, but, as Brian had pointed out the night before, there was nothing wrong with being the star at your own wedding, as long as you remembered who was the real star in the rest of your life. Every now and then, during the eating and the speeches and the cutting of the cake, Stanley felt a stab of worry about his forthcoming initiation into the physical side of marriage, but there were too many immediate distractions for such concerns to seriously affect the happiness of the afternoon.

The wedding night itself turned out to be rather tentative and incomplete, but Stanley and Alison had read some good books and received a lot of excellent advice on matters relating to sex. They knew that these things took time, and would be that much better in the long run if qualities of patience and mutual sensitivity were faithfully applied to their ongoing development as sexual partners. Certainly, as the years passed, they did achieve a quiet compatibility, punctuated infrequently with moments when something more vital seemed to happen.

Once, only half waking in the middle of the night, Stanley had made love to Alison in the sleepily mistaken belief that she was a completely different person altogether. That encounter had been suffused with such passion, drama and midnight music in the velvety darkness, that both of them lay quite stunned and motionless afterwards, staring up in the direction of the ceiling, unable to find any clue in their experience of each other to solve the mystery of what had just happened. In the morning Alison's eyes shone, and she sang in the shower, but Stanley felt guilty and frightened. He resolved that such a thing would never be allowed to happen again. Dreams and real life had no business overlapping.

Mark was born, much to the delight of Stanley and Alison and Alison's mother and Brian and Madge (who had promised to take on god-parent roles in the child's life), on the anniversary of his parents' wedding. Brian joked with Stanley about the expense and hard work that would be involved on that day each year. Mark was a robust, contented baby, whose favourite thing was to stare with bright, curious, gently flicking eyes at a butterfly mobile bought for him by his Nanna. Every now and then he would break into a gurgling chuckle and wave his chubby fists at the gently moving coloured shapes. Stanley sat and stared at Mark for hours sometimes, hardly able to believe his good fortune, and wondering where on earth or heaven his little son had come from.

Two years later, Ruth, a sister for Mark, was born early one beautiful morning in springtime. She was small with a great pile of fine, dark hair and impossibly miniature, almost transparent hands and feet. Later, looking at the tiny figure lying naked in his arms, Stanley realized two things: that love does not become thinner because it is spread further, and that he knew nothing at all about women.

By the time Stanley reached his late thirties the Morgans had been able to move into a larger house with a back garden more suitable for young children. Money was not plentiful, but it was more than adequate, and the family was beginning to establish its own traditions and routines, a development that particularly pleased Stanley because he did like to know just where he was with everything. Quite often, when he was absolutely sure there was no one else about, he would sit on one of the wooden bar stools in his kitchen at home and run through a check-list of the important things in his life, naming them out loud, and reassuring himself as he went along, that each element was safe and functioning healthily.

Wife, son, daughter, God, church, house, job and physical health – these were the components of Stanley's existence that had to be oiled and serviced regularly, as it were. He was painstakingly conscientious in his attention to each one of them, and grateful to God for helping to make his life run so easily. He secretly played with the idea that there was an element of reward in his good fortune. After all, he had hardly put a foot wrong since the incident on the common all that time ago. Having said that, he knew – of course he did – through the teaching he'd received over the last few years, that it was impossible for anyone to actually earn his or her way into good favour with God. Of course he knew that. Of course he did. Still – everything was working out extremely well.

Then something happened.

One of the very sensible decisions that Stanley and Alison had made together was about walking the children to school in the morning. Stanley was able to work a flexi-system as far as his hours of employment were concerned, but because the Land Registry was quite a long way away, he had to choose whether to leave later in the morning and see the children before setting off, or go to work very early and see them at the other end of the day before they went to bed. After considerable prayer and discussion it was agreed that Stanley would, for the time being at any rate, begin work at ten o'clock, thus allowing time for him to walk Mark and Ruth the three-quarters of a mile from home to school each morning. Stanley, in particular, felt strongly that this daily half-hour of contact would prove to be very important in developing the right kind of relationship between himself and his children, and Alison was pleased because it gave her a head-start with 'getting on', the phrase she used to describe her housework.

For some time Stanley had no cause to regret the decision that he and Alison had made. Ruth was a bright, incessantly chattering little girl, who trotted happily along with her small hand in his big one as she communicated her views on life, school and the world in general, never seeming to doubt that her father was paying close attention to every word she said. Mark, a serious child, but no less contented by nature now than he had been as a baby, walked on his other side, speaking infrequently, but usually asking deep and thoughtful questions that resulted from a great deal of preliminary pondering, on those occasions when he did have something to say. Sometimes the two children would speak to him at exactly the same time, each appearing to regard the conversation of the other as background noise which could be reasonably and cheerfully ignored. Stanley became rather good at punctuating his carefully considered replies to Mark with enthusiastic nods and appreciative noises in the direction of his daughter, who needed little else in the way of response to maintain her small but freely-flowing stream of consciousness.

After only a few days Stanley found himself really looking forward to his regular morning walk. He basked in the sunshine of his children's affection and closeness, experiencing a quiet (but surely innocent) pride in the picture of happy Christian family life that the three of them must undoubtedly be presenting to passers-by.

It wasn't until this pleasant morning ritual had been going on for several weeks that two disturbing patterns began to emerge.

There were bound to be patterns, of course. Mornings had to be timed properly. Stanley and the children set off each day at exactly eight-thirty, arriving at the gates of Park View Junior School just after ten to nine, in order to leave nice time for Mark and Ruth to relax for a few minutes, greet classmates, and say goodbye to their father before two loud blasts on a whistle signalled the time to line up and go in.

On every single week-day morning between eight-thirty and ten to nine, Stanley and Mark and Ruth passed children and parents walking in the opposite direction on their way to Whitefields, another junior school (definitely an inferior one in Alison's estimation) situated only a few hundred yards from the road where the Morgans lived. After a few weeks Stanley was able to predict with consistent accuracy the time and place at which he and his own children would encounter quite a selection of these Whitefields parents and pupils, none of whom was known to him by name, as they happened to be neither friends nor members of his church. After waving goodbye to Mark and Ruth and setting off for home, he would, at equally predictable intervals, meet most of the same people during the walk back. It was the pattern of daily encounters with two of these fellow parents that began to disturb his life.

The first was more of an irritant than anything else, but, as the days and weeks went by, it increasingly spoiled Stanley's enjoyment of the whole of the first half of his walk to school with the children. This early part of the journey involved a long, dead-straight section of pavement running along the side of a main road which, at this time of the morning, was frantically busy (Stanley had insisted from the beginning that the children should hold his hands particularly tightly as they negotiated this potential hazard). It so happened that, almost every morning, as the Morgans rounded the corner opposite the garage (Mark and Ruth tightening hands automatically as they embarked on this three-hundred-yard stretch) another little family group of two very small boys and their father would come into view at the other end of the footpath. At first, passing each other and their charges with difficulty on the narrow pavement, there had been no more than an exchange of politely rueful smiles between the two fathers, a silent acknowledgement that they were colleagues in mild adversity. So frequently did they encounter each other, however, that the nature and quality of these regular exchanges grew by infinitesimal degrees each day, until, eventually, the two men were greeting each other with the familiarity and warmth of old friends.

Stanley hated it. He hated turning the corner each morning, only to see the tall, skinny figure with the prematurely greying hair appear at the other end of the road, with his two robin-shaped children toddling along on either side. What were you supposed to do with your hands and your face and your body when there was a one-hundred-and-fifty-yard walk between you and the point where you would meet the person you were walking towards, and you were visible to each other for the whole of that expanse? At what point did you begin the greeting process? If you began to smile too soon it would look as if you believed the relationship had a significance that it didn't actually have at all. But how could you avoid catching someone's eye too early in the course of a long, straight, uninterrupted walk like that? You couldn't. Not unless you gazed with inexplicable interest at the path, or your feet, or the traffic, or the brick wall that ran beside the pavement for almost the whole, eternal distance.

Stanley found himself building up an extensive collection of activities to fill the void. Looking at his watch was one, suddenly taking a deeply concentrated interest in what one of the children said was another. Occasionally, he even stooped (literally as well as metaphorically) to unnecessarily untying and retying one of Ruth's shoelaces, to the little girl's slight bewilderment. This was a good one, as it could be stretched to last very nearly half a minute, quite a chunk out of the endless eye-catching time that had to be filled somehow.

Stanley's misery was only increased by a growing realization that the other father was finding the whole thing just as excruciatingly difficult as he was. He observed covertly that the tall grey man had developed ploys of his own. On more than one occasion, for instance, he had plucked some very ordinary-looking leaf from the bushes that grew over the top of the wall and studied it with frowning concentration for fifty yards or so, and then, as if submitting to clamorous requests, he had bent down to show it to his patently uninterested sons, tapping and pointing and explaining, seemingly so engrossed in the joy of imparting knowledge that he completely failed to notice the impending Morgans. Once, he had taken a comb from his pocket, and, before applying it to his sons' immaculately tidy hair, spent some moments moving it carefully around in his hands, as though the imbecilically simple task of checking that the teeth were pointing outwards rather than inwards required a great deal of serious thought.

At the point on the path when the two families actually met, Stanley and the grey-haired man would, with apparent suddenness, become aware of each other for the first time that morning, exchanging chappy pleasantries with a relaxed geniality that was certainly in direct disproportion to the way that Stanley, and probably the other man as well, actually felt. The return journey was blessedly free of a similar encounter, as the grey-haired man, much to

Stanley's relief, must have gone on to whatever work he did after dropping his children at school.

One Saturday, in the local supermarket, whilst doing the weekly shop with Alison and Mark and Ruth, Stanley, to his horror, found that they were directly behind the grey-haired man, his children and a lady dressed in a tracksuit who was presumably his wife, in the check-out queue. When their eyes met both men displayed bright and instant pleasure at meeting so unexpectedly, but neither of them attempted to introduce the other to their respective wives, and the grey-haired man hurried his family away as quickly as possible after paying their bill.

When Alison asked who the man was Stanley didn't quite know what to say. His problems with those morning encounters happened on a level of consciousness that he would have had the greatest difficulty in communicating to himself, let alone his wife. He frowned and smiled as if a little puzzled and apologized for not effecting introductions. He said that he knew he'd met the man somewhere, but couldn't remember where. Later, as they had their after-shopping drink and doughnut in the cafeteria, little Mark announced solemnly, after a great deal of cogitation, that he thought the man in the queue might be someone they met on the way to school sometimes, and Stanley said, oh, yes, now he came to think of it, that was probably right, and he was surprised he hadn't realized it before. Well done, Mark!

After returning from church on the following day, Stanley sat on his usual chair at the kitchen table drinking coffee while Alison prepared Sunday lunch at the other end of the room. Feeling that her husband was unusually quiet, Alison asked if anything was wrong. Stanley said, no, there was nothing wrong, but he'd been thinking about the mornings and walking the children to school, and had more or less decided that the time had come to change his work hours so that Alison could spend that special half-hour with Mark and Ruth each day. In fact, he continued, he had sensed during the service just now that he was being directly led into such a decision. Stanley believed what he was saying even though he knew it to be quite untrue.

Alison was extremely surprised to hear this suggestion for such a radical change of routine in their lives. She pointed out mildly that they had always prayed together in the past before making big decisions, and asked what was different about this time. Stanley became quite irritable for the first time since their marriage, spluttering incoherently about Ephesians and husbands and wives. Alison cried a little into the potatoes, and, then, with a sudden flash of intuition, asked if all this had something to do with the grey-haired man they'd met in the supermarket yesterday. At this, something short-circuited in Stanley's system. He banged his fist angrily on the table, rushed out of the kitchen and ran upstairs to his bedroom where he lay on his back staring up at the ceiling, hardly breathing as he tried to understand what was going on. There was something happening deep inside him, right under the surface, something to do with the morning walk and the grey-haired man, and yet nothing at all to do with him, and yet, something about the feelings inside him – was he in love with the grey-haired man? Panic-stricken, Stanley rolled across the bed, physically removing himself from the place that had been occupied by such a preposterous notion. Of course it was a preposterous idea, but he *was* in love with someone – something. Hugging his knees to his chest and closing his eyes tight he found himself sinking into a green darkness filled with sweet, tearful sadness. There was a face just visible in the shadows. Beautiful, seductive eyes – eyes that looked at him for just an instant before turning away. Where had he seen those eyes, not just once, but often – almost every day? Suddenly he knew.

Stanley got off the bed, washed his face in the bathroom, dried it and his hands on his favourite big, blue fluffy towel, took a few deep breaths and went downstairs. He explained to a very worried Alison that he had been feeling a little tired and things had got a bit out of proportion. He was really sorry that he had upset her so much, and he hadn't meant it about the morning walks. They should have lunch as usual and forget what had just happened. Alison was very pleased that things were back to normal, but the incident had frightened her. Later, she asked if Stanley felt that he might like to go round and visit Brian and Madge that afternoon. Perhaps they could pray together that whoever or whatever had attacked their happy lives before lunch would stay away in future. Knowing that he wouldn't, Stanley said that he might well do that, and the rest of Sunday was peaceful.

That night Stanley lay awake for hours, full of worry and guilt and excitement, thinking about the thing that had really been disturbing him about his morning walk to school with the children. Until today he had somehow managed to pretend that nothing was happening at all, but now, there it was, right in front of his mind. It had been invisible, but now he couldn't make it go away even if he tried, and he didn't know what to do about it. He tried to think clearly, hoping that if he teased the thing out into its component parts it might look insubstantial and silly, and perhaps just go away.

It was a woman. It was a woman who was not Alison. It was a woman whose identity was as much of a mystery to him as that of the grey-haired man. Stanley had never spoken to her. She had never spoken to him – not with words, anyway. It was a woman who walked her daughter to Whitefields School each morning, just as the grey-haired man walked his sons. He knew she must start out later than the grey-haired man, though, because she didn't pass Stanley and the children until they reached the line of fir trees at the top of the school lane, just after turning right by the roundabout. Stanley tried to picture exactly what the woman looked like, but apart from a vague impression of colourful clothes, dark, glossy, shoulder-length hair and very shiny black shoes, he found it very difficult. He realized that he had never quite dared to look directly at the woman.

Her eyes were the only part of her that he was absolutely sure about. As he thought about them a trembling ripple seemed to pass through the entire length of his body. Those eyes were – well, they were so large and long-lashed and inviting, so full of something he had always ached to have, without knowing what it was or even whether it really existed. Stanley knew, as he lay there in the dark, that he had thought about nothing but the woman's eyes for weeks and weeks.

It had begun in such a small way. The woman happened to glance up at him as they passed on the pavement one morning, that was all, but, even at that ridiculously early stage, he had, with a sudden inward little gasp of wonder, seemed, just for an instant, to see in her eyes the possibility of finding his way through or down into a different kind of world, a warm, dreamy place that he had given up all hope of ever visiting, let alone inhabiting. It happened again the next morning, and the next. It happened on every school-day morning.

As the days went by that little flick of a glance had seemed to increase in duration, until now, every morning, the woman's eyes held his for what must surely be a fraction of a second longer than was appropriate for two strangers passing on a footpath. Then, on the way back, he would pass her again, but this time she would be walking much more quickly, and her eyes would be very deliberately averted, almost as if, he told himself, she realized the danger of making any sort of contact when their respective children were not there to act as a buffer of respectable restraint. She might well be lying in the dark herself at this very moment, perhaps thinking about Stanley and wishing, as he wished, that – that what? Stanley closed his eyes and rolled his head from side to side in a reluctant attempt to dispel the wrongness from his mind.

How on earth had he managed to convince himself that it was the business of the grey-haired man that had disturbed him so much? Was he going mad? Was he possessed by some evil force or spirit that was twisting his mind and trying to turn him into a different kind of person? A light perspiration broke out on his face and forehead as he considered this possibility. Turning his pillow over he rested his cheek on the coolness of the other side. What should he do? Time to send Jesus to the door? But even as he asked himself the question he guessed that this particular matchstick model had no chance of surviving tonight. He was right. It was smashed and swept away by the flood of what he was feeling and wanting. And the confusing thing, the really confusing thing, was that right in the centre of this overwhelming torrent of dark and sinful feelings, Stanley could have sworn that he detected a small, shining wave of absolute rightness. How could that possibly be? He must be mistaken. He must be!

All of this night-long worrying and thinking and teasing-out resulted in one thought only. Stanley knew what he wanted now. The desire of his heart was entirely visible for the first time. He couldn't wait for the morning to come. He couldn't wait to see those eyes again.

Next morning the encounter with the grey-haired man was a different matter altogether. From the moment the single tall figure and two small ones appeared in the distance Stanley kept his eyes firmly fixed on the other man's face, determined that he would not flinch for any one of the following one hundred and fifty yards. He succeeded, and greatly enjoyed seeing his fellow parent thrown into a state of mild panic as he was forced to employ an even greater variety of avoidance strategies than usual. At the point where they actually passed, Stanley produced one small, utterly self-contained smile, and was rewarded by an expression of puzzled embarrassment on the face of the other man, who had automatically launched into the over-familiar greeting mode that both of them usually used.

Now it was nearly time for *her*. In not much more than one minute's time he would see the woman who was making his whole being buzz with excitement and anticipation. Unconsciously, he took his hand from Ruth's and passed it across his hair. He pictured himself cleaning his teeth earlier that morning and was glad that he had. He drew himself to his full height as he walked, instead of allowing the top half of his body to incline towards the children and their conversation as he normally did. Mark and Ruth were both chattering happily away now, although he had absolutely no idea what either of them was talking about. It was very nearly time. Just a few more yards and there she would be.

Perhaps, this morning, he would let some very small indication of his feelings show in the glance that he threw her when they met, just the merest hint of an acknowledgement that he knew what was going on between them, and that he wanted something – whatever that something turned out to be – to happen.

Suddenly, as they turned the corner, there she was, hurrying along past the fir trees towards the roundabout with her daughter. She was there! Stanley tingled with yearning and a sudden nervousness. How was it going to be possible to convey all that he wanted to communicate in one small glance? If he attempted to inject a new significance into the look he gave her was it not possible that he might accidentally transmit aggression or annoyance, thereby repelling rather than attracting her? Stanley quivered with frustration. He had such scant experience of dealing with the opposite sex. Studying the toes of his well-shined shoes as he walked, he tried out a variety of expressions in the hope that he might hit on one that seemed exactly right.

They had started to walk round the curve of the roundabout now, and, by a rough estimate, were likely to encounter the woman and her daughter at a point thirty yards down from the top of the road that eventually led to the school. If he timed it correctly, Stanley reckoned, he should be able to lift his head and look into her face just as he and the children passed the first of the fir trees that stood on their left after they had turned away from the roundabout. Taking a deep breath, he checked the distance quickly out of the corner of his eye. Yes, a few more yards – say, ten of the reduced strides he had to do on the way to school because of the children's shorter legs – and then it would be the ideal moment.

It was as Stanley actually began to count down from ten to nought, that young Mark decided he really did want an answer to the important question that he had asked three or four times already without getting any response at all from his distracted parent. Raising his voice as he asked the question yet again, the little boy began to tug rhythmically at the sleeve of Stanley's jacket, hoping to wake his daddy up from the dream that he appeared to be in as he strode along making faces at the pavement.

Stanley was furious. Only seconds to go before the most important thing in the world happened, and this irritation had been set up just to deprive him of one little moment of happiness. He felt a savage anger towards its perpetrator, but for now he ignored his son, gritted his teeth, and continued to count down towards nought. At 'three' Ruth compounded her brother's offence by pointing out in her high and infuriatingly clear 'helpful' voice, that Mark was trying to ask him a question.

Postponing a reaction to either of his children, Stanley reached 'nought' in his counting before raising his head. And yes. Yes! Oh, yes! There it was. There they were. There were the eyes. There was the only question that truly interested him. There was the promise, the invitation, the possibility of being soaked and absorbed at the same time; the prospect of sinking through deep, warm waters, in which to close one's eyes and drown would be nothing but a pleasure. There, too, was a slight curve of the soft, full lips, a coquettish smile that was as good as an extended hand. He didn't remember ever seeing the smile before. Now, he would look forward each morning to the smile as well as the eyes. As for all his practised expressions, he had used none of them, but he was quite sure that his soul had been in his eyes. She knew. She must know.

After passing the woman and her daughter, and when he was sure they were out of earshot, Stanley turned on his children with a fury that frightened both of them and made Ruth cry. It was the first time they had seen him lose his temper, let alone get so *very* angry. He said that he didn't think it was too much to ask that he should be allowed a little peace in the mornings when he walked them to school, and that he would answer questions when he wanted to, not at a time when it just happened to suit Mark. As for Ruth, the whole thing was nothing to do with her and she should mind her own business and not shout in the street. He added that if Mark ever pulled his jacket around like that again when he was busy thinking about something important, he would most likely give him a smack. Did they understand? Mark and Ruth nodded miserably, not understanding at all. The rest of the walk to school was conducted in virtual silence. Stanley was too excited to feel guilty yet.

After depositing the children, Stanley set off on the journey back to his house with a light step and a rapidly beating heart. In less than five minutes he would see her again and – well, who could say what might happen? Anything was possible. In fact, when he did pass the woman as they negotiated the path by the roundabout in opposite directions, she hurried past him as she had always done when they met on the return trip, except that, this time, although she hardly glanced at him at all, that small curve of a smile appeared on her face once more, and Stanley knew with a further little lift of his spirit that it could only be intended for him.

From that morning, and for the following two weeks, the Morgan household seemed to Alison like a ship that has run into perilously stormy weather, and is in serious danger of sinking without trace or being wrecked against jagged rocks. She really was at her wits' end. Over coffee with Madge while Stanley was at work one day, she tearfully asked how anyone could change so much and so suddenly. Since nearly two weeks ago, everything she said and did seemed to infuriate him beyond measure. It was almost as if, she explained, her very existence annoyed him. He acted as though she ought to be feeling guilty about bothering him by being in his life at all. She had wondered if something was going wrong at work, but when she very gently mentioned that possibility, he had told her so witheringly that she was being about as stupid as it was possible for a human being to be, that she'd burst into tears, and that had irritated him even more. He couldn't stand her crying at the moment, which made things especially difficult because that was what she felt like doing most of the time.

Madge gently asked Alison what she had done to try to improve the situation. Alison described how she had determined to be patient, knowing that Stanley must be going through some sort of dreadful crisis, and that it couldn't really be anything connected with her. She'd tried things like preparing his favourite meals at suppertime, but apart from perfunctory thanks he hardly seemed to notice the effort that she made. She'd tried hard to look attractive and be more interested and interesting in the evenings, thinking that perhaps Stanley was beginning to find the unvarying sameness of people and places each day weigh heavily on him, but all her attempts to start conversations and show that she cared what was happening to him provoked the same tone of weary exasperation in his voice. She was beginning to dread that tone. In fact, she told Madge, every single attempt she'd made to improve the situation had failed before it was given a chance to begin working, and she was running out of ideas.

Madge wanted to know how Stanley had been with the children. Not as bad, Alison told her, but even though he was making more of an effort with them (he still seemed keen to walk them down to school each morning, for instance) he was much snappier and quick-tempered than he'd ever been in the past.

In addition to all these things, Alison said, Stanley was tending to come to bed much later than he ever had before, and when he did eventually arrive he would turn his back on her in such a pointed way that she had stopped trying to make any contact with him at night for fear of his anger and rejection. All in all, the situation was just horrible, and she was getting so worn down with it that she didn't know how much longer she could carry on.

Madge asked if it was likely that Stanley would agree to see Brian for a chat and maybe some prayer? Alison explained that Stanley was 'off' everyone in the church at the moment, but she decided not to tell Madge how, as well as speaking in a very negative way about the church in general, Stanley had made some very sarcastic comments about Brian in particular, describing Madge's untidily dressed husband as the 'Shambolic Shepherd', and declaring that he was planning to take an indefinite holiday from everything to do with church.

The two women prayed together for a little while, then Madge departed, leaving Alison alone, lonely, and desperately wishing that everything could hurry up and go back to the way it used to be.

Stanley, meanwhile, was plunging wildly from invigorating sensations of being fully alive for the first time, to intolerable extremes of guilt when he dared to think about the unhappiness that would be caused to others if the dreams that filled his head at the moment were ever to come true. But he was trapped inside what he wanted. He wanted the woman with the beautiful eyes. He knew that. It was like a fever in him. She somehow represented the fulfilment of a promise that had been made to him by – by whom? He didn't know. He just knew that he had a right to something connected with her, even if it turned out not to be the woman herself. He had a right.

On the second Saturday following the Monday when he had established his dominance over the grey-haired man, Stanley drove the twenty miles into Cambridge to buy a new carpet-sweeper. Alison had asked if she and the children might come with him so that they could all go to the pictures and have something to eat out, but he had clicked his tongue and sighed and looked so put out by the suggestion that she had given in straight away and said it didn't matter.

All the way to Cambridge Stanley thought about the woman with the beautiful eyes. The weekends were such a waste of time. He never saw her at any other time but weekdays. All he wanted was for Monday to come so that he could meet her on the way to school and on the way back, and see the little smile that he now felt was specially his. Nothing else had happened. Perhaps nothing else ever would happen, despite the variety of passionately hopeful scenarios that he rehearsed continually in his mind. But it might. Roll on Monday.

He bought the carpet-sweeper in a large electrical store next to a garage and a supermarket and a cinema on the edge of town. It was as he was about to go out of the shop, carrying the new sweeper in a big cardboard box, that he met the woman with the beautiful eyes just as she was coming in. She was not alone. Behind her, shepherding the little girl he was used to seeing with the woman on every week-day morning, and followed by a dark-haired boy of about fourteen who was the image of his mother, came a tall, friendly-looking man who could only have been her husband.

The woman stopped when she saw Stanley, and gave a little amused laugh before she spoke.

'Good morning. Isn't it funny how you don't think people exist outside the times when you're used to seeing them? Darling, this is a man whose name I haven't got the faintest idea of, whom I meet every single day of the week on the way to school with Suzie. Man-I-meet-every-day-of-the-week-without-knowing-your-name, this is my husband, David, and these are Thomas and Suzie.' She glanced at his purchase. 'And we all hope you'll be very happy with your new Hoover.'

After he had introduced himself and a few more pleasantries had been exchanged, Stanley said polite goodbyes to each member of the family and returned to his car, carefully stowing the new carpet-sweeper along the back seat. After closing the rear door he stood quite still for a moment, staring across the tops of the other cars.

The woman with the beautiful eyes had been bright and witty, probably not a Christian, but certainly the sort of person one could very easily like. The rest of her family seemed to be the same. Pleasant people. Perhaps he and Alison could get to know them. Maybe they could come to dinner one evening when Brian and Madge were there as well. That would be really nice.

He locked the car and set off in search of a public phone. There was a whole row of them just outside the supermarket. One was free. He inserted a twenty-pence coin, punched in his own number and waited, listening to the ringing tone. At last, Alison's voice, laden with trouble, said, 'Hello, Alison Morgan here.'

'Hello, Ali,' said Stanley, 'it's only me.'

'Stanley! Where are you?'

'Cambridge, of course. I've just bought a Hoover.'

'Oh, right! Good. So, what did you…?'

'It wouldn't be too late to bring the children up on the train, would it? If you came now. I could meet you at the station.'

'Well, yes, I could, but I thought…'

'Let's take them to the pictures and then have a cream tea. What do you think?' Silence. 'What's the matter?'

'Nothing – sorry, I was just so pleased that you wanted us to…'

'Don't be sorry, Ali. Listen, get a move on now and come up, and then when we get back, and the children are safely in bed, let's light a fire in the sitting-room and lock the front door and bring that thick rug down from our room and make love on it in front of the fire.'

'On the rug in front of…? Stanley Morgan!' She sounded far more pleased than shocked.

'Yes, on the rug – the one I chose – the green one.'

Posthumous Cake

Granny Partington died just before eleven o'clock on a Wednesday morning in the middle of the greyest, drizzliest October there had ever been. She caused as little trouble in her dying as she had done in her living. The little self-contained unit, specially built on to the side of her son's house, was as clean and cosy and friendly as it had been since she first moved in with all her bits and pieces ten years ago. There had been no long distressing illness, despite the fact that Granny was only a week short of her ninetieth birthday, and all her important papers, including a will that carefully divided three hundred pounds into four legacies of seventy-five pounds each for the children, were neatly bundled and beribboned in the small roll-top desk next to the television.

Rachel Partington had been shopping on that Wednesday morning. She came straight from the car to the annexe with Granny's old cloth bag in one hand and a half-wrecked umbrella clutched optimistically in the other. Coffee with her mother-in-law was not a duty for Rachel. Mum was the only person who accepted her for what she was. They were best friends.

As she stood in the tiny porch, wrestling her umbrella into subjection and flapping out of her son's absurdly large wellington boots, Rachel chattered happily.

'I got you a *Mail*, Mum, 'cause all the *Expresses* had gone, and I found a really nice bit of beef in the cheap trolley – nothing wrong with it at all. Oh, and you do have to sign the form yourself, they won't let me do it. If you sign it now, Bob can pop it in when he gets home, and…Mum?'

No comfortable response noises. No oohs and aahs of warm appreciation and reassurance. No flap of slippers on the kitchen floor. No clink of coffee cups and saucers (Mum couldn't abide mugs). No rush of water into the old tin kettle. No Granny sounds at all.

Rachel found her best friend lying on the bed in her slip, one hand cradling her powdered cheek on the pillow like a child. Later, Rachel wondered why she had been so certain that Mum was dead.

'I just knew,' she said to Bob that afternoon, 'and I... I lay down next to her on the bed for a minute and said goodbye, and cried for a while. It sounds silly, but I wished I'd stayed in the porch for ever, pulling those ridiculous boots off. Oh, Bob, I didn't even have a chance to give Mum her shopping, and it was such a lovely little bit of beef...'

Everyone was in for tea that day, but it was a very quiet meal to begin with. They had all heard by then.

Lucy, the youngest, kept staring into the far distance, her four-year-old brows knitted with the effort of understanding what 'no more Granny' could possibly mean.

Benjamin was eighteen. He had many strong and radical views, but Granny Partington was not an aspect of life. She was a safe place – a secret repository for his trust in human beings. Inside, he wept like the weather.

The twins, Frank and Dominic, had suspended hostilities as soon as they heard about Granny, both of them crying openly, one at the top of the stairs and one at the bottom, curled up like hampsters with their grief. Frank was still sniffling now, as he sucked orange squash through a plastic straw and ate his beans and sausages. Dominic was white and quiet. He ate and drank nothing. The twins were nearly ten.

Rachel looked across at Bob. He was being very strong and supportive with everyone else, but there was a greyness about his cheeks and mouth that she hadn't seen since Lucy had come so close to dying in hospital three and a half years ago.

Rachel stood up. It was time. 'I've got something to show you all,' she announced. Reaching into the larder behind her, she took out a jam sponge on a plate and placed it in the middle of the tea-table. 'Look,' she said, 'Granny made a sponge for us. I found it in her cupboard. She'll have made it this morning.'

'It must have been the last thing she did.' Bob's voice broke very slightly for the first time.

'A posthumous cake,' murmured Ben.

'Can we have some?' said Frank.

Rachel sat down, picked up a knife and began to cut the sponge.

'I'm going to cut it into six pieces,' she explained, 'so that we can have one slice each. But no one's allowed to eat a single crumb until they've reminded us of one special thing about Granny.'

Silence fell. Six pieces of cake lay untasted on six plates. Granny's sponges were famous in the Partington universe. Like so many cooks of her generation, the old lady had produced these delicious creations by throwing what appeared to be randomly measured handfuls of ingredients into a bowl, stirring them up a bit, then sticking the mixture in an oven. The results were always perfect. This was the the last one they would ever eat.

'I know a special thing about Granny,' said Frank. 'She gave us two pounds on our birthdays, and we always knew it was a lot.'

Rachel smiled and nodded. Granny had always put two pound coins in an envelope for each of the children when their birthdays came, and because everyone knew that two pounds was a lot for Granny to give, they treated it as a big and important gift. It was one of the things that had reassured Rachel about her children.

'She was very good at enjoying things, wasn't she?'

'What do you mean, Ben?' asked his father.

'Well, she always thought everything was really nice and sort of sparkly. If you bought her a cup of tea when you were out it wasn't just an ordinary cup of tea, it was a *wonderful* cup of tea. And if you were walking somewhere she noticed all the flowers and the houses and the people. I dunno, she was just good at being happy. Not many people are, are they?'

'Aren't they?' enquired Lucy, who was a very happy child. 'I thought they were.'

'What do you remember most about Granny, darling?'

'I'm not saying this just because I want to eat my piece of cake, Daddy.'

'Of course not, sweetheart.' Bob spoke solemnly.

'What I remember most about Granny is her cuddles. She loved me,' added Lucy, looking around proudly.

'Her face is like that puff-pastry stuff,' mumbled Dominic, unexpectedly. 'I squeeze it hard with my hands, and she says "Go on with you, you'll squash my nose off", and we laugh and she gives me a biscuit.' A huge tear rolled out of the little boy's eye and dropped with a plop on to the plate beside his piece of cake.

Rachel put her arm round Dominic's shoulders and rested her face on the top of his head. 'The thing I shall always love about Granny,' she said, 'is that she never made me feel useless and silly, even though I am useless and silly a lot of the time. She made me feel good. I'll miss her so much – we all will.' She paused for a moment. 'Bob, you haven't said anything.'

He stirred and spoke. 'I was just thinking – while you were all saying those excellent things – that I've always used Granny as a sort of ruler, a kind of measure, I suppose. Granny loved all of us, but she loved Jesus as well.' He stopped and looked at Ben for a moment. 'I know some of us aren't quite sure what we think about all that at the moment, and that's all right, but she really loved him and she lived her life the way she believed he wanted her to. Every time I went to a talk or heard a sermon or read a book about what we ought to do or how we ought to feel, I used to think about my old mum. She didn't talk about it much, but she lived it. They won't ever put her in one of those Famous Christian books, but she *was* it. She was *doing* it as well as it could be done, I reckon.'

'Can we eat our cake now?'

'Course we can, Lucy,' said Rachel. 'We'll all eat our cake now.' She looked at the ceiling. 'Thanks, Granny.'

'Thanks, Granny,' echoed everybody except Dominic.

Nobody said anything else until the last mouthful of sponge had been eaten. Then Frank pointed at the plate in the middle of the table.

'There's some little bits left, Dad,' he said, his brow furrowed with the effort of trying to remember something important, 'aren't you supposed to eat it all up before you wash the plate?'

'You're thinking of something else,' said Ben.

'No, he's not,' murmured Rachel, as her husband collected the remaining crumbs and put them in his mouth.

Father to the Man

It was very difficult to sleep after seeing my son so distant and miserable that evening.

I was still awake at two o'clock in the morning, having read almost half of *Biggles And The Black Peril* to take my mind off the dreadful bleakness in Dan's eyes as he said goodnight. Violet had always hated me using my old children's books as emotional teddy bears, but I couldn't think of any other way to cope with the feeling of hollow panic that arrived with the night.

Eventually, worn out by tiredness and the constant effort needed to keep the image of Dan's face away from the front of my mind, I left Biggles, Algy, Ginger and Bertie to their own world-saving devices and drifted off to sleep. It seemed only seconds later that I was awakened by the sound of the bedroom door opening.

'Daddy,' said a small frightened voice from the other end of the room.

I sat up. My daughter, dimly visible in the half-darkness, stood just inside the doorway, a fluffy friend clutched firmly under each arm. Her feet, two little frayed ends, were brightly lit by a narrow shaft of yellow light from the streetlamp outside the landing window. Curly wasn't too big to be helped, and wouldn't be for a long time. I could give her everything she needed on this particular night.

'Hello, darling,' I said softly, 'what are you doing here?'

'I woke up an' was a bit scared of the dark, Daddy.'

'Come and get in with Mummy and Daddy, sweetheart. We won't be afraid of the silly dark then, will we?'

The feet disappeared as Curly pattered across the two yards between her and the bed, clambered up with a helping hand from me, and threw herself into the gap between Violet and me like a soldier jumping into a fox-hole.

'Is that Curly?' mumbled Violet sleepily. 'Are you all right, my love?'

'Bit scared, Mummy,' said Curly, taking her thumb out of her mouth to speak, then putting it back again.

'Well, you're okay now, aren't you, Curly-Poops?'

Curly nodded briskly on the pillow as Violet kissed the back of her head before turning over to go back to sleep. I lay awake for a while watching sleep and safety chase away the fear from the little girl's face. Finally the sucking motion ceased, Curly's thumb dropped from her mouth and she began to breathe deeply and evenly. The darkness had been defeated once more.

It could be Danny lying there, I thought, as I studied Curly's serene features by the light filtering through the curtained windows above the head of the bed – it could easily be Danny lying there. It had been Danny many times when he was a little boy, when he was as openly vul-nerable and frightened as his sister had been tonight, when Violet or I could solve just about every problem he was likely to face with a cuddle or a distraction or one of those academic explanations that he enjoyed so much, when he was Danny instead of Dan, and his life had seemed so happy that I really wasn't able to see how he could be anything but content when he grew older. I had poured so much of myself into that child – the best of myself. Me without the manipulation and the sulking and the subtle neglect that I had been capable of in all my other relationships. How could he not be all right now, when I had given him so much then? Was I going to go through it all over again with Curly when she was older? Grief and pain passed through me in waves as I waited for sleep to come.

'I find it very difficult to forgive Dan for being unhappy.'

That was the remark that got the following day off to such a bad start, and I suppose I knew, if I'm honest, that it wasn't going to go down at all well with Violet. She had been up since about six-thirty with a very excited child. Curly's eyes popped open every morning like bubbles bursting. She saw no point in wasting a single moment of any of these wonderful days, that happened like magic again and again, on dozing or lying awake in bed. Besides, today was one of her two play-group days, and Valerie, the lady in charge, had promised they would do finger-painting on Thursday. Today was Thursday. What joy! Curly had been sharing this joy of hers generously with Mummy for two and a half hours by the time I made my bleary-eyed way downstairs to the kitchen. Violet was slumped over yesterday's paper and a depressing-looking piece of toast when I made my opening statement. She didn't even look up when she replied.

'I don't mind getting up with Curly and seeing Dan off to school while you're doing your corpse impression upstairs, but I do object to playing audience when you talk like some third-rate Oscar Wilde. If you're trying to convince me that you're a writer, then I suggest the most persuasive argument would be a sheet of paper with something actually written on it. You'll still have a couple of working hours left today if you take half as long over breakfast as you did yesterday.'

I almost fell over. I never had been able to handle Violet's ability to slice me in half with words when she really wanted to. Various replies chased each other round my mind. I wanted to point out that I had talked like a fourth-rate Gilbert Chesterton, not a third-rate Oscar Wilde. I wanted to tell her that I had a brilliant idea for a comic novel, so well developed that I could begin writing it today. Most of all, though, I wanted to tell her that I really had meant something when I spoke just now. It was true that I had spent some time preparing what I was going to say as I washed and dressed and hid my Biggles book, but that was only because I needed to invest my vulnerability with a little dignity. If I'd let my feelings out in their raw, undisguised form I might have ended up on the floor sobbing my eyes out. No one had ever seen me doing that, and Violet was not going to be the first. Nevertheless, I wanted her to know that I really was feeling bad. I dropped a slice of bread into the toaster.

'I wasn't just trying to be clever, Violet, I was quite unhappy last night, you know.'

Leaning back, Violet pushed both hands heavily through her hair before answering.

'Dan is a perfectly normal teenage boy, Paul. Last night he revealed that he's going through some of the perfectly normal problems that perfectly normal fifteen-year-olds go through. There's no tragedy about him getting a bit low sometimes. He's growing up and changing, that's all.'

'I know that, but...'

'What you're really talking about is you. You can't accept that your relationship with him is changing as well. You can't solve everything for him any more and neither can I. Why should we expect to be able to? You don't want him to be some sort of pre-adolescent dependent for the rest of his life, do you? Or perhaps you do. Well, I don't!'

'Of course I don't want...'

'In fact, if anything, Dan needs you and me even more now than he did before. He's unsure about who he is or where he's going. He needs us to be strong and support-ive in the background, not feeling sorry for ourselves because he's failing to make us feel good in the same way. I'm sorry if you feel I haven't let you be unhappy, but I think you've got to face reality for Dan's sake.'

Violet would have been astonished if she had known how close I came to collapsing emotionally at that moment, how near she was to hearing about the feelings of desolation and bereavement that were crippling my peace since Dan opted to continue his journey without my close and intimate companionship, and how impotently furious I was that the battle raging inside me between adult and child was depriving my son of the kind of father he needed so much at the moment.

'Anyway,' said Violet, 'I must go to work. Your toast is done. I'll see you later.'

'So, who,' I asked nobody in particular as the front door shut behind my wife, 'do I talk to about feeling more miserable than I've ever felt in my life?'

Locked, as I was, into my own failure to communicate, it seemed impossible that such a question could ever be answered satisfactorily.

I didn't write anything for the rest of that day, although guilt kept me at my post until the hour when your average respectable working man would feel it right to down tools.

People who have never written for a living find it very difficult to understand the most pressing daily problem for scribblers. The plain and awful fact is that, on every single working morning, you must freshly create a universe which will distract, enthral or otherwise absorb you to the exclusion of all the real, day-to-day considerations that are tugging at your attention. This 'universe' simply doesn't exist until you construct it yourself out of ideas and inventions that can be found only in your own head, and not, sadly, at any shop in the High Street.

As I sat at my study window, a piece of A4, feint-lined, narrow-margined paper leering emptily up at me from the desk, my head was full of Dan, and the gap that seemed to have opened up so abruptly between us. I fantasized conversation after conversation between him and me, in the course of which all was healed and settled and restored to the sweet and sunny way it was. Pain filled me as each imaginary dialogue ended, and the false relief that it brought ebbed away to reveal the stomach-lurching truth that was robbing me of peace.

I had one consolation. It was a book recently presented to me as a sort of symbol of friendship by my best friend,

Greg Parker, a reluctant coach-driver, who suffered, as I did, from advanced cricket mania. *The Book Of Cricket* by Plum Warner was a rare prize unearthed by Greg in the local second-hand bookshop. Published more than sixty years ago and containing a rich mixture of fact, opinion and photographs, this satisfactorily fat and faded volume was almost as powerful a distraction as Biggles, and represented an act of heroic sacrifice on my friend's part. Greg valued and studied our relationship as misers do their gold, and he liked to celebrate it from time to time with the sort of gesture that had resulted, last week, in my ownership of this treasure. He had brought it to the pub at the usual time on Friday wrapped in very carefully chosen paper, presenting it to me between our first and second pints, and saying only, 'I thought this might appeal to you.' Inside the front cover he had written:

> *To Paul, a gift from your friend Greg.*
> *May we continue to speak the truth to one another.*

Reading a paragraph or two from Warner's book every now and then and peering at the quaintly posed, old-fashioned action photographs did bring some relief from my feelings, but I found myself coming back again and again to that inscription on the title page.

Central to the friendship between Greg and me was the mutually accepted and frequently stated fact that we always told each other the truth. Nothing was too dark, shameful or distressing to be withheld, because we were prepared to own each other's problems. In the same way, any joy or good fortune that occurred to one of us was invariably shared and celebrated by the other, usually at 'The King's Head', which was our regular meeting place on Friday evenings.

Perhaps because I was unusually sensitized on this particular afternoon, I became aware of something I had known, but never managed to acknowledge before, namely, that this so-called 'fact' about our relationship was not a fact at all – not as far as I was concerned, anyway. I had no doubt that Greg had been unsparingly vulnerable and open in his dealings with me. All through the long period when his ridiculous marriage had been falling to pieces, for instance, he had shared personal problems and insights into his own behaviour that I knew I would have had the greatest difficulty in even mentioning to anyone at all. Many of our Fridays still consisted almost entirely of Greg describing and analysing and seeking reassurance about aspects of his life and personality that had been troubling him during the week just past. All that was really required of me was the occasional nod, a few encouraging noises, a round of drinks when it was my turn, and the vaguest of vague acknowledgements that we were very similar people, and that, therefore, I couldn't fail to understand exactly how he felt.

Somehow, I had managed to avoid sharing any important part of myself with Greg, and yet, if you had asked him how well he knew Paul Williams, he would have smiled happily and said that he knew everything there was to know about me. Greg's marriage had been of the type that scatters previous friends like some sort of social hand-grenade, and its failure after five years had left him lonely, lost and severely lacking in self-confidence, so I knew how important I was to him, and for reasons of my own I valued the need he had for me.

Sitting there at my desk, holding the token of friendship that he had given me, I realized for the first time how much Greg's dependency had become part of my own security. I enjoyed and looked forward to that sensation of hiding inside my head on Friday nights, secretly feeding his mistaken belief that we were genuinely close. It was cosy and unchanging. It made me feel tall and deep and relaxed and wise. I felt sorry for him, and gave myself little pats on the back for tolerating such a sad character. It was suddenly borne in upon me that I even enjoyed the occasional flush of annoyance that I felt on those evenings when he'd spoken about himself solidly for an hour and a half, without ever seeming to feel it necessary to ask how I was, or how my life was going. Not that I would have told him much if he had asked. I would have made some general, fairly whimsical point about the problems of being a human being, and set him off again with a question carefully designed to trigger a new monologue on strictly Greg-related subjects. It was easy to manipulate him.

Violet's response to my friendship with Greg was resigned, but slightly scornful. She said that I was using him to postpone genuine contact with people, and that I should invite others to join us on a Friday night to prevent both of us from getting away with the pointless games we played with each other. She was probably right, but she didn't really know how cataclysmic a revolution like that was likely to be.

I didn't want any revolutions tonight. I wanted business as usual. I wanted to take my misery about Dan down to 'The King's Head' and hug it to myself as I listened to the list of problems that Greg was likely to produce. I felt quite excited, in fact. There was something about the effects of a couple of pints of beer that ennobled misery, and allowed a mellowing of the sharp emotions that were so unbearable in a strictly sober state. Yes, that's what I'd do – float sadly along on an underground river of melancholy, bravely withholding the pain that my needy friend would be unable to cope with if I exposed it to him.

My disappearance to the pub each Friday was usually preceded by an uneasy passage of arms with Violet. If I had worked well and productively during the day I was quite confident in my casual announcement that I was 'off to the pub' for the evening, but if, as was the case on this particular day, I had actually produced nothing at all, then my carefree cry had a hollow ring to it. Unfortunately, Violet had a very discerning ear.

'You would say that you had earned the price of an entire pint today, would you, Paul?'

That's what she said – always a new line from Violet, who should have been a writer herself – and, as usual, it had the effect of gutting me. I laughed, but it came out sounding squeezed and unconvincing. Then I felt confused. There was anger boiling up in me, but was I right to feel angry? There was hurt, but was genuine hurt a justification for doing no work at all for an entire day just because I was a soppy writer? If I'd been a roadmender I'd have just gone and done it, wouldn't I? But then, why shouldn't I go for a drink with a friend once a week – I mean, why not?

'It wasn't a bad day,' I lied, adding more truthfully, 'I need to go out tonight.'

But she wasn't going to say the magic words of permission: 'Off you go, then. Have a good time. Don't drink too much…' I had to leave heavy-footed, with the sour taste of disapproval in my mouth, but it only lasted for a few hundred yards. After that I began to sense the inward effects of that first pint lightening my step and drawing me onward. Soon I would be sitting opposite Greg at the corner table that we had pretty well made our own. There I would cuddle my private chaos and he would express his. I almost skipped as the coloured lights of the pub came into view around the next bend.

Nothing could have prepared me for the double shock that I experienced when I finally entered 'The King's Head' and glanced expectantly in the direction of our usual table. Greg was certainly there, but he was not alone – that was the first part of the shock. He was engaged in earnest conversation with a man I'd never seen before. The second was when he suddenly spotted me and hurried across, his face shining as though the dusty old forty-watt bulb inside his head had been replaced by a new hundred-watt one, to grab my arm and whisper in my ear.

'Paul, it's fantastic!' breathed my poor, unhappy, dependent friend, 'you've got to come and meet Steve and let him tell you what he told me. Paul – it's *so* great – I've become a Christian!'

Have you ever experienced the feeling that a vital supporting wall in your life has suddenly collapsed? That's how I felt as I followed Greg back to the corner table in the saloon bar of 'The King's Head'. What a betrayal of our relationship if he actually had made a move into some kind of commitment or belief with absolutely no reference to me, and without any thought of how our friendship might be affected. And what in God's name was all this 'come and meet Steve' business? If the wretched individual who was now rising and extending a hand towards me was really responsible for poor Greg's new delusion, then he was the last person I wanted to meet. How could my so-called friend have brought him here to *our* place without at least giving me some warning? Everything in me tightened and tensed as I took the hand that was offered to me. I gripped it more tightly than necessary to show who was boss. He spoke first.

'Hi, my name's Steve – I work with Greg. He's been telling me that you two make a habit of this.'

Steve was an ordinary-looking sort of bloke, quite tall, dark-haired, casually dressed and with a pleasant, crinkly smile, although I wasn't very interested in the pleasantness or otherwise of his smile at that particular moment. I decided to regard his comment as a critical one.

'A bad habit, you mean?'

'Not at all.' Steve's smile was undimmed. 'Jolly good habit, if you ask me. I wouldn't mind getting into the habit myself. Sit down and join us. Can I get you a drink?'

Like a sealed kettle I bubbled with silent fury. How dare this man invite me to sit down at a table and in a place that were more mine than his? I set my face in what I hoped was an expression of calm and steely independence – and sat. Yes, he could get me a drink.

'Okay, I'll have a pint of Directors and a large scotch chaser with nothing in it.'

He didn't turn a hair, damn him. 'Directors and a large scotch with nothing in it – right. What about you, Greg? Have another shandy?'

'Shandy!' I couldn't believe my ears. I laughed with exaggerated harshness. 'You're drinking shandy? Please tell me I'm dreaming!'

Greg blushed purple.

Steve spoke easily. 'What d'you usually drink, Greg? I'm only having shandy because I like it. You have what you want.'

'He drinks Directors like me,' I said sardonically, 'at least, he did up to last Friday. I'm not quite sure what's happened since then.'

'Pint of Directors, Greg?'

Greg nodded, his face still flaming, as Steve set off towards the crowded bar.

For a few moments neither of us spoke, then Greg leaned forward over the remnants of his small Christian shandy and spoke pleadingly.

'Paul, I know you're feeling stroppy because there's someone else here and all that, but everything's changed, and…'

I hated him being right about how I felt. I interrupted as crudely as I could.

'Greg, just tell me what's happened, and please, please promise me you haven't brought that man along here to convert me, because if you have I'm going home right now, if not sooner.'

The excitement that had been lighting up my friend since I first saw him a minute ago was far stronger than his embarrassment over the drinks. I couldn't remember a time when I had seen such life in his face or heard such animation in his voice.

'I've asked Jesus into my life, Paul! I've been born again!'

So loudly did Greg make this appalling announcement that the whole bar went quiet for a second or two. Then several people laughed and the noise level returned to normal. I didn't know where to put myself. I could have died.

'You don't have to shout your head off about it, do you?' I hissed. 'The whole bloody pub knows about it now!'

'Yes, but isn't it great!' hissed back Greg in a horribly penetrating whisper, looking like a kid who's just been given what he wanted for Christmas. 'I've never felt so good – Jesus has saved me!'

'No, it's not great,' I replied, with cold, intentional cruelty, 'it's sad – pathetic. You've let some Bible-bashing loony get you all worked up about something that doesn't exist, and now you want me to have my brain washed so that I'll end up as demented as you. You were just the same when you got talked into that pyramid selling thing a couple of years ago – that lasted about ten days as far as I can remember. It was going to be *the* answer, remember? All your money problems were going to be solved within a month. It was just as obvious then that you'd been taken for a ride. Let's face it – you're easy meat for these dream-merchants, Greg. They must think it's their birthday when they see you coming.'

Greg's face clouded over. Good. He was still within my reach. He looked at me like a puppy the first time it's been smacked.

'You told me you thought that was a good idea at the time,' he said. 'Didn't you mean it?'

'Of course I didn't mean it,' I snapped, hating myself, 'but sometimes you have to let people find out for themselves that they're up the creek. You wouldn't have listened if I had told you what I thought. People don't.'

Greg looked at me with his head on one side and said nothing for a little while. The expression of slowly dawning comprehension on his face made me want to grab all my words back and pretend that I'd never said them. Sometimes, though, when, for better or worse, you set out on a new way, you can almost hear the sound of gates clanging and locking behind you. Maybe all roads were going to be new ones from now on.

That bulb was suddenly switched on inside Greg again as he remembered his new faith. I just felt plain, bright-green jealous.

'Paul, believe me – this really is different.' Greg clenched and unclenched his fists with the frustration of being unable to convey the passion that he felt. 'When Jesus...'

I couldn't stand it any more. I spoke through gritted teeth. 'Greg, will you stop saying that word! I have to be absolutely honest with you – it makes me feel physically sick in my stomach. I don't know why, it just does. It's so – yukky! And you sound so stupid when you come out with it.'

Steve reappeared with a tray. 'Pint and a scotch for you, Paul – one for you, Greg. And some crisps. Sorry it took a little while. Cheers!'

My first gulp from that first pint was *so-o-o-o* good. It slid down my throat like a rabbit running from a hound. I concealed a sigh and relaxed a little. Greg sat and stared at his beer, blinking in thought. Nobody said anything for a moment or two.

'Penny for 'em,' said Steve at last, placing his glass carefully down on to a mat on the polished surface of the table.

Greg looked up abruptly as though he'd suddenly regained consciousness. 'I was just thinking,' he said, 'about how different people can be. Paul was just saying while you were up at the bar that hearing the word Jesus makes him feel really sick, and ever since Tuesday evening it's made me want to cry with happiness every time I say it or hear someone else say it. Isn't that weird?'

Steve looked at me with nothing but calm interest in his expression. 'That's how it makes you feel, eh?'

I was none too pleased with Greg for repeating what I'd said. There are things you say to stir your friends up that are way too excessive to be passed on to anyone else. Embarrassing. Still, in for a penny, in for a pound. I'd show this smoothy God-follower that I wasn't a push-over like Greg. I finished my pint in one long swallow and downed a good third of the whisky.

'I'll answer your question when I've got myself another beer,' I said, standing up with my empty glass in my hand. 'What about you two? Ready for another one?' Childishly, I injected the merest trace of contempt into my tone as I glanced at Steve's half-full glass, and Greg's pint of Directors that, incredibly, hadn't even been started yet.

'I'm okay, thanks,' smiled Steve, 'you carry on, though.'

'Oh, I shall do,' I muttered to myself under my breath as I made my way to the bar, 'I shall carry on whether you give me permission or not, thank you very much indeed.'

Waiting at the bar, I tried to analyse the nervousness that had crept into me. There was something about this bloke Steve that was threateningly unflappable. I knew how shaky I was inside over the whole business of Dan, and I didn't want to be prised open in some way by the conversation that was about to take place. I'd just have to be careful. When I was served at last I had a secret extra whisky to give me confidence before returning to the table with my fresh pint. To my annoyance Steve and Greg were speaking quietly with their heads close together when I got back. They stopped talking as I sat down, and Steve turned to me with that same imperturbable smile.

'Right,' he said, 'you were saying – about Jesus.'

I drank the other two-thirds of the whisky in front of me before replying.

'I was saying that the name of the person you claim to follow makes me feel physically sick.'

My words climbed out of my mouth with the exagger-ated clarity of incipient tipsiness. Those first three drinks had gone down far too quickly. I was still just about in control, though, and beginning to feel rather clever. Thank goodness Violet wasn't here. Greg looked expectantly at his new friend, trustingly convinced that some kind of lofted spiritual straight drive would smash my secular full-toss for six. But Steve just nodded his head in an interested sort of way, leaning back and considering for a moment before he spoke.

'Mmm, I fancy you wouldn't be alone in thinking like that.'

Bastard! I wanted to be alone in thinking like that, not just one of some boringly predictable crowd who all felt the same about everything. Still, if he was determined to make himself feel safer by placing me in some common atheistic category or other, I'd make damn sure I represented my 'group' as forcefully as possible. I took another mouthful from my glass of bitter and licked my lips.

'Why, does that surprise you, then?' I asked, with what I hoped came over as nonchalant scepticism. 'I really don't see why it should. As far as I can see the church is a place where people who are already nearly dead go along to practise being completely dead for an hour or so every Sunday. No wonder the bloke who started that makes people feel ill. Pathetic state of affairs, I'd say, wouldn't you?'

I was rather pleased with this little speech. The stuff about nearly dead people was really quite good. I glanced at Greg to see if he was impressed, but he was wearing his dying frog expression, staring at Steve as if disappointed that Steve's straight drive had been intercepted and caught with such ease by the bowler. Excellent! With a bit of luck this whole situation could be normalized before too long.

'I'd have to agree with a lot of what you say,' said Steve. 'There are loads of churches like that, but not all, by any means, and I don't think that actually explains why people react so strongly – almost violently – to Jesus himself. I mean, you were talking about feeling physically sick, weren't you? That's a very extreme way to feel, isn't it? What do you think are the real reasons for you being so violently anti-Jesus?'

I opened my mouth as if I couldn't wait to answer, but actually I was quite pleased when Greg broke in before I had a chance to speak. I hadn't wanted to look as if I was stuck for a reply, but the truth was I had no idea what I was going to say.

'Drink up, Paul, I'll get you another one. Steve? No? Same as before, Paul? Right...'

Greg's early enthusiasm was ebbing away. I had the distinct impression that he was trying to prevent or at least deflect our conversation from the course that it was taking. Perhaps, I thought, he was worried that his new hero, and consequently his new faith, could crumble under the onslaught that I might be about to unleash. As Greg disappeared into the crush around the bar, Steve made an encouraging gesture with his hand.

'Carry on, Paul. You were about to say...'

'I'll wait for Greg,' I said, my manner suggesting that Steve was trying to cheat in some subtle way.

Another silence fell. I didn't know what he was thinking, but I was trying to get my brain into some sort of reasonable gear for negotiating an answer to the question that I'd just been asked. It was nice to have two fresh drinks in front of me when Greg got back. After these two I was quite likely to get silly, but I still had enough control left for one major speech. I sipped carefully from the overfilled pint glass and wiped froth from my top lip with the knuckle of a forefinger.

'Steve's into cricket like us,' said Greg somewhat plaintively. He must have known perfectly well that we weren't about to embark on a friendly discussion of last summer's batting averages.

'Hold on, Greg. Steve asked me a question. It's bad manners not to answer questions. Why am I violently anti-Jesus? – that was it, wasn't it? Okay, well – here goes.' I counted the points on my fingers. 'First, he was a failure. Getting nailed up on a bit of wood at the age of thirty-three can hardly be counted as a winning move, can it, especially if you've been claiming to be God and have miraculous powers? Secondly, it hasn't worked, has it? It's caused more wars and trouble and torture and killing than just about any other movement in history. Thirdly, as I was saying just now, people who do call themselves Christians seem to specialize in being boring or hypocritical, or both. And fourthly...' I felt the muscles in my hands and face contract as I searched for words to express the only genuine problem on my list, 'I dunno – there's something so mealy-mouthed and...and cringingly gruesome about this goody-goody wafting around in a dress like some hippie, telling everyone that life isn't important and we've all got to be nice to people we don't like. It all seems so weak and spineless and useless. That's why most people despise him, I should think. It's why I do. He was just a pathetic twit. Does that answer your question?'

Another silence fell. Steve seemed to be peering down into his drink, so I couldn't see his face. Greg was sitting upright, fingertips on the edge of the table, staring at me in disbelief, as if I was a complete stranger. When Steve looked up at last I searched his face for a reaction. It didn't take much searching. Not so imperturbable now. His eyes were wet with tears. What on earth was going on? I felt uncomfortable suddenly, hot and heavy and crass, like a child who's experimented with a dirty word without knowing what it really means. Perhaps I'd been a bit harsh. But then, I told myself, I hadn't started any of this. All I'd done was come out for a drink with my best friend, and found myself confronted by this shandy-drinking, scaled-down version of Billy Graham. No, I had nothing to feel guilty about.

'Well, you did ask me,' I said, 'so I told you. Being a Christian you wouldn't want me to tell anything but the truth, would you?'

Steve shook his head slowly. 'No, you're absolutely right, Paul,' he replied quietly, 'I'd much rather you said what you really thought.' He paused for a moment. 'Do you...do you mind if I tell you why I got a little upset?'

Unwisely, I downed the whole of my third whisky in one gulp. Sledging in the dark from now on. I shrugged my shoulders with studied unconcern, last of the great democrats.

'Fair enough.' A bit slurred. 'I've had my slay – say, you have yours.'

I looked at Greg. He was a dismal lump, hunched miserably over his drink. For a fleeting moment I thought *I* was going to burst into tears. Too much alcohol, I thought, that's all it was.

'I got upset, Paul, because...well, because the things I believe are not just a set of ideas or a way of living or anything like that. For me it's all about the Jesus that you think of as a spineless twit.' He raised a hand to ward off objection. 'No, I'm not complaining about you telling the truth. You only said what an awful lot of other people think.'

Bastard!

'No, the thing is that...well, I love him, you see. I love Jesus. I don't just believe in him, or think he made some good points, or told good stories or any of those things. It's gone way beyond that. I really love him, and when you were saying about him being weak and silly I felt like crying, because he's here and he's listening, and he's had two thousand years of being despised by the...the people he did so much for. He wasn't weak, Paul. He was strong and obedient, even though it meant dying in the end. And can you imagine how his father felt?'

'God, you mean?'

'Have you got any sons, Paul?'

The wound inside me opened. I answered in a whisper. 'Yes, one son – called Dan.'

'Can you imagine how your heart would break if Dan was separated from you because of what other people had done? All that father's love raging with pain and grief until he was safely back with you again. Because that's what happened with Jesus on the cross, and it's still happening over and over again when people can't see what he's done for them. That's why I got so upset, and I can't help it because it means everything to me.'

The light had come back into Greg's face in the course of this speech, and now, as Steve stopped speaking, he turned hopeful, expectant eyes towards me. I put my empty beer glass down, knowing that I had only enough sobriety and self-control remaining for one reasonably coherent piece of communication. I spoke slowly and distinctly.

'Could I please ask you to do something for me – both of you?'

They nodded. Greg leaned forward eagerly.

'Would you please go away – right now, without saying anything else, and just leave me alone.'

They sat and stared at me for what seemed like a long time, but then they did go. I stayed and got very drunk. At around eleven-thirty I somehow managed to get a coin into the slot in the phone-box outside the pub.

'Violet, c'you come and pick me up?'

'Literally?'

'Please.'

'Start staggering and I'll meet you half-way.'

I've often felt wrecked, but not usually on every possible level. I woke up on the Saturday morning with a hangover in my heart as bad as the one in my body. Physically, mentally, emotionally and spiritually – whatever that might mean – I felt coated and streaked with the indelible marks of some species of shame. I tried to wash it away under a scalding shower, but that only woke me up a bit and made me even more conscious of my wretched self. Hot, sweet coffee revived me to an even higher level of dismal awareness, and four pain-killers cleared my head just enough so that I could begin to focus on how miserable I really did feel. Violet had said almost nothing when she picked me up from the pub after closing time the previous evening, but, like good old Biggles when bandits appear at two o'clock, her mouth had been set in a thin, grim line. I knew that the reckoning was to come. After an eternal night spent in a bed half occupied by my indignantly malfunctioning body, and half by the silent mass of disapproval that was my wife, I was not looking forward to the weekend.

There was one small mercy. By the time I dragged myself downstairs, Violet had taken Curly to her swimming lesson, and Dan was nowhere to be seen. I presumed that he'd taken himself off to his Saturday job at the local Eight Till Late shop. I had the house to myself for an hour or so. Thank God!

'No, don't thank him,' I muttered to myself, 'he doesn't exist. And if he does, he's not very nice. He causes trouble between friends.'

I made some more coffee and tried to work out what I was going to say to my wife.

I was still sitting at the kitchen table when Violet and Curly arrived back. Dear Curly burst through the front door and rushed along the hall towards me with undisguised joy, throwing her arms around my neck and kissing me on the cheek.

'I did really well at swimming, Daddy! Mummy says I'm doing the breathing for the crawl exactly right now and we had a slushy drink and a chocolate biscuit afterwards 'cause I didn't take too long getting changed. What have you been doing? You should have come, Daddy. Daddy should have come, shouldn't he, Mummy?'

Enthusiasm and innocence worry and disarm me.

'I wish I had come, Darling. I love watching you swim. Perhaps I'll be able to come along next...'

'Daddy looks very *tired*, Mummy,' interrupted Curly solicitously, placing her hands on my shoulders and drawing back to study the puffiness under my eyes and the general limpness of my demeanour. 'He does, doesn't he, Mummy? Poor Daddy looks ever so tired. Why don't you make him a nice cup of tea?'

I avoided my wife's sardonic eye.

'Yes,' said Violet dryly, as she filled the kettle and plugged it in, 'poor Daddy does look rather tired, doesn't he? But he may not want anything else to drink this morning because he did rather a lot of that last night, didn't you, Daddy? Perhaps that's what's making you so sleepy today. *Shall* I make you a cup of tea now, or do you think you'll be too tired to drink it?'

'Err, yes,' I replied, 'thank you very much, Violet. That would be very nice. Curly, darling, why don't you take a drink and a biscuit into my study and do me a really nice drawing of your swimming class, eh? I'd like that.'

Curly pretended wide-eyed puzzlement. 'I can't draw a picture with a drink and a biscuit, Daddy. You have to use colours.' She went into peals of laughter at her own brilliant joke. 'Can I use your special pens just this once?'

'Yes, make sure you put the tops back on each time you finish with one, though, won't you?'

'Course I will.' Sensing that her absence was being bought, Curly decided to up the price a little. 'Can I use your very, very special paper as well, if I don't waste it, please?'

'Yes,' said Violet firmly. 'Shoo! Here's your drink and your biscuit. Now go!'

Curly departed serenely, aware that our unwritten contract involved her staying out of the kitchen for at least a quarter of an hour or so.

Violet placed tea in front of me and sat down at the other end of the table. I studied the flower design on my mug with narrow-eyed, intense concentration. This very satisfying item of unusually thin china was the sole remnant of a batch of four we'd unexpectedly come across on an East End market-stall a few months earlier. Both of us preferred our hot drinks in this particular mug. The difference between Violet and me was that, whereas when *she* made the drinks she always gave me the good mug, when I made them I usually awarded the prize to myself, and the chipped Manchester United mug to her, or else she got the one that was annoyingly small with a handle too little for your finger to go through. After Violet had pointed out this difference to me a few weeks ago the flowery object had become to me a sort of symbol of my own self-ishness. Ever since that day I'd made a point of always giving my wife the nice mug, but I didn't really want to – I just wanted to claw back a little of my self-esteem.

There's a limit to the time you can convincingly spend staring at mug designs, however pleasant. It was time for me to say something.

'Better get the shopping done, I suppose.'

This sparkling conversational ploy was a pathetic attempt to steer Violet's thinking away from the specific subject of my drunkenness the night before, and the current, general cloud of gloom that was suspended immediately above my head.

'Why did you get drunk last night?'

I can never decide, when a row is brewing, which of various possible options to select. Self-justification usually springs to the front of my mind before anything else, but this can be very hard work, involving, as it does, the racking of memory to recall occasions when Violet has committed similar or equally heinous crimes. She doesn't commit many. Nor was it as if I could plead stress due to an excessively heavy work-load. My output had dwindled to almost nothing recently, despite quite a reasonable flow of commissions. There was always the 'I'll do what I want – you don't own me, you know' tack, but such a response is easier in theory than in practice. Violet was more than capable of dealing with that one. Less devious, but certainly potentially more dangerous, was the option of exposing real resentments – genuine, unresolved feelings of hurt that would be heavy enough to club my wife's complaints about drinking out of existence. Something inside me still trembled with child-like rage over the way Violet tended to shut down my agony about Dan because it wasn't quite rational enough for her liking. I didn't really want to go down that road at the moment. Where might it end?

I decided to opt for a kind of truth.

'I got drunk last night because Greg's become...well, he thinks he's become a Christian. He's got religion. I don't know how you say it. He's met this bloke called Steve something-or-other, who was in the pub with him last night when I got there, and all they wanted to talk about was Gentle Jesus, Meek and Mild, who drinks shandy rather than bitter.'

My voice was full of scorn, but I suddenly realized that if my attitude to Greg's conversion really had been as dismissive and laid-back as I must be sounding now, there was little if any justification for my claim that it had precipitated my descent into inebriation. I was right. Violet put a finger to her chin and moved into Perry Mason mode.

'Let me see if I've got this right. Greg's had some kind of religious experience which you – despise? Is that too strong a word? I want to get this right.'

I shrugged. 'Yes, more or less, but...'

'And he came along with the man who talked him into this despicable state, or led him there, or whatever, and on hearing about this you immediately had no choice but to get expensively, stinkingly drunk. Is that a fair summary of what happened?'

'No-o-o!' I went through my tongue-clicking, head-shaking, sighing routine. 'It wasn't that. It was just that...well, he was making such a fool of himself. You know what he's like when he gets an idea into his head. Nothing else matters for a week or two, and then suddenly he loses interest and he forgets he ever was interested. He's always been like that. Remember the shopping thing

– the pyramid selling thing? That was almost like a religion. He just gets taken in so easily and – I don't know… It upset me.'

'So why didn't you get drunk on the night when he told you about the pyramid thing?'

'Because,' I explained, speaking with great clarity as if to a half-wit, and dropping blindly into the pit I had so efficiently been digging for myself, 'like I've already said, I knew it wouldn't last.'

'Whereas this time…?'

I stared at Violet in silence for a moment, and then, to my own horror, a sob burst from me and I started to cry.

I imagine that people who cry easily in front of others will find it hard to understand why this was such an earth-shaking experience for me. The fact was, though, that I had been brought up never to display excessive emotion in front of anyone. For me, the idea of shedding tears in a public place, even in such a limited and domestic public place as the presence of my wife, was the equivalent of walking naked along a crowded street. Violet and I had, for a variety of not very good reasons, avoided open discussion on the subject of my repressed nature for some years now, although I knew that it was a source of great sadness to her that I so rarely expressed affection, and virtually never shared other, deeper feelings.

My little sob of grief was, in fact, so unprecedented in our relationship, that neither of us knew what to do next. I pulled myself together almost immediately, but the damage, if that was what it was going to turn out to be, had already been done. I have to confess that the detached observer in me, the sharp-eyed watcher who saw all new experience as potential writing fodder, waited with interest to see how Violet would react to such an unusual display of emotion. The other me, the one who had lost control for a second, was horrified that she should have seen me in such a vulnerable state, no matter how brief that glimpse had been. I took a few deep breaths and said nothing while she stared at me with a warily puzzled expression on her face.

I was struck suddenly, and for no particular reason that I was aware of, by how much I still secretly loved my wife's face after years of marriage. I loved her large, dark, serious eyes, and the way her mouth kinked humorously at one corner, and her handsome grown-up nose and the way her dark hair tumbled in ringlets on to her shoulders. I wondered for the thousandth time why I was incapable of telling her things like that, when it would have assuredly been *such* a very good thing to do.

She said nothing for so long that, in the end, I couldn't meet her gaze any more and had to resort to further mug-studying.

'Paul...' Violet took in a deep breath and blew it out again like a stream of cigarette smoke before speaking quite gently. 'What is all this really about?'

I found that, unconsciously, I'd begun a slight backwards and forwards rocking movement in my chair, perhaps trying to establish some sort of pattern in the midst of chaos. Now I had to decide whether or not to make contact with Violet. How about a postponement? I looked up at her.

'What is all *what* really about?'

She twisted back in her chair, and, after considering me appraisingly through narrowed eyes for a moment, seemed to make a decision, one which to my troubled perception had 'RISK' written all over it. She leaned forward, resting her folded arms on the table, and spoke just as gently as before.

'All right, if you're really asking me, I'll go through it, and you can tell me where I'm getting it wrong. Work, first of all. You're doing hardly any writing at the moment, which would matter very much if it went on for a long time, for obvious reasons, but only matters at the moment because it shows that your mind is so busy wrestling with something else that you can't concentrate.

Okay, so what exactly are you wrestling with? Well, we know part of the answer to that, don't we? You've been very upset lately because Dan, in common with almost every other boy of his age who ever lived in the entire universe, has decided to experiment with the idea that he exists in his own right. What does that mean? It means that he's trying to move on to centre-stage of his own life, and *that* means that you – and me, if it comes to that – are relegated to new, equally important but purely supporting roles while he sorts himself out in the starring one. Like I said, that's upset you a lot.'

Yes, Violet, all the things you say about experimenting and existing and centre-stages and supporting roles are very, very true, but you haven't actually understood because you're not down here inside me. He was my little, big, growing friend, Violet. He was the only person I've held in my heart like a poor man holds a diamond given to him by a God who's actually there. He was the only toy I never broke or damaged. He was the one project to which I gave everything, without trying to cheat or cut corners. He was the best thing I've done. He was the hope that I might not be hopeless. He was the only mirror I ever wanted to look into. Down here in the dark, Violet, there's a lot of wailing and crying and agony going on. The pain, Violet, it's like a pneumatic drill thundering away inside my head. It doesn't let anything else happen. Excuse the jumble of mixed metaphors, Violet, but it's like the bloody Arctic – endless night, and I'm sick with fear that there aren't going to be any more mornings. Not real mornings where everything's all right after all, and the sun shines like in a picture book, and absolutely anything could happen, and you laugh at the things that frightened you when it was dark and we're all happy ever after. Violet, Violet, Violet, do you really not understand? Won't you come down here into the dark with me and hold me and look after me, just until the morning comes...

'That has upset me a bit, yes.'

'A bit?'

'Oui, un morceau.'

Silence. Dilated nostrils. A determination to persevere just in case it should turn out to be worth it.

'Shall I go on?'

'I like your hair.'

Silence. Incredulous little shake of the head. Last chance, no doubt.

'Just now, for the first time since we've been together, you cried. Only a little bit. You packed it all back in the box straight away – as soon as that tiny fragment escaped, in fact. But it was there, Paul. I saw it. Something about this business with Greg and whatever it is he's got himself into has really got under your skin, hasn't it? It actually made you weep in front of me. Paul...'

I had renewed my china examination, but something in the quality of the ensuing pause made me look up. Violet's eyes were filled with an unusual softness now, her voice gentler than ever.

'Paul, please believe me – I *want* you to share your feelings with me. I know you think I don't understand and don't really want to support you, but have you ever faced the fact that you never actually tell me how you're feeling? What I mean is – have you realized that I get shut out from the part of you that cries? You know what's going on inside you, but I don't. How can I? I was pleased just now when you...when you got upset. No, that's not true. I wasn't just pleased. Paul, I felt a little twinge of excitement. We've lived in our own worlds for such a long time now. I've been so lonely. If you only knew how much I want us to be close...'

Her eyes begged me. I could see her waiting for me just out there on the outside. But though I shook the bars and kicked at the walls and shouted and screamed with all my might, I couldn't get out.

The thing is, Violet, that when Greg brought that man to the pub and said he'd got converted, and messed up our Friday evening – well, that wasn't fair, was it? I mean, that's our time – Greg's and mine. Our place. And he belongs to me. Greg belongs to me, not to a man called Steve who's all calm and nice and Christian. I mean – if I've got to lose Danny, surely I don't have to lose Greg as well, do I? Violet, I haven't got many people, you see. I can't go on losing them because in the end there won't be anyone left. That's why I cried. You'll stay with me, won't you, Violet? You won't let anyone take you away, will you? I couldn't bear that. Apart from Curly I'd be on my own, and I'll probably lose her as well, one day. Hold me. Please, hold me…

I heard my voice starting to speak, but I couldn't stop it.

'Ah, well, the reason for my tears is quite simple. I'm suffering from an illness that the doctors have only just properly classified. It's called P.P.M.T.T. which stands for Pre-pre-menstrual-tension-tension. It's a married man's thing occurring for about a week in every month, and it's invariably followed by another condition known as Post-pre-menstrual-tension-tension. The symptoms commonly include a quite uncontrollable desire to imbibe alcohol, and a tendency to burst into tears for no reason at all. I'm afraid that at these times we men are hopelessly at the mercy of our wives' hormones.'

There was no softness in my wife's eyes now, just distance, deep, deep disappointment and a strangely flavoured fear that chilled my heart.

'I'm going to go and see to Curly,' she said, and she went.

'I love your eyes,' I said, too quietly for her to hear.

Saturday lasted for about a decade. The day after drinking too much usually does. One is dismally aware that the chance of recovering enough physical or mental energy to actually enjoy anything more demanding than television is very slim indeed. Added to this general slump was the realization that any irritation on my part would be construed (with complete accuracy, of course) as a symptom of my recent alcoholic extravagance, and condemned accordingly. I went to bed early that night and fell fast asleep almost immediately.

Waking early on Sunday morning, I found my mind full of thoughts about Greg. Later today, I conjectured, he'd be getting up and dressing as smartly as he could (given the rather cowboyish nature of his wardrobe), then setting out with this new excitement of his to whichever church old smoothy Steve was part of. My whole body twitched involuntarily with embarrassment as I imagined my old friend and drinking partner explaining publicly how his heathen friend had reacted so negatively to the news of his conversion. Oh, God! They'll probably pray for me, I thought. Someone will ask the Lord to break through the barriers of doubt and resistance, and all that garbage. Sickening!

I turned my head to one side expecting to see Violet's head on the pillow and the dark shape of her body silhouetted beside me, but she wasn't there. For one wild moment I was full of breathless panic. She'd gone! Violet had finally had enough and left me in the middle of the night, taking Dan and Curly with her. I was on my own and I didn't even know where my family were. A moment's calmer reflection suggested that incest among the Waltons was marginally more likely than my wife doing something so disruptive and potentially harmful to the children. Violet's appearance at this point with a mug of tea (it was the nice, flowery mug) seemed to confirm this view. But why had she brought me tea this early in the morning? It was unlikely to be a gesture of affection.

'I've already been up for ages, worrying my head off,' said Violet, placing the mug down on the table beside my bed, 'so I don't see why you shouldn't wake up now. You and I have got some very serious thinking to do, and I suggest you get started on it right now. I can't carry on like this, and I don't intend to. Something's got to happen, so you'd better start asking yourself what it'll be. I'm going back downstairs.'

The cold, unyielding, mechanical quality in Violet's voice made my heart sink like a stone. I reached a hand out towards my tea, but drew it back as a wave of unhappiness passed through me. What on earth could I do about being me? I couldn't just decide to be a different kind of person, could I? Or was that silly and self-indulgent? Perhaps what was really required was for me to make a much greater effort to set aside my own stupid Pavlovian emotional responses and think about what others needed from me. Could I grit my teeth and tough it out? The trouble with doing that, as I knew full well, was that eventually I was bound to run out of motivation and no longer be able to resist the temptation to advertise my selfless heroism. And if that revelation didn't provoke enthusiastic and prolonged applause I just *knew* that I would descend into sludgy self-pity, and things would probably be worse than before. Perhaps counselling would help...

I'm not sure how I managed to drop off to sleep again at about that point in my thinking, but I do know that I drifted into a very vivid and disturbing dream.

In my dream I found myself back in the pub, except that it wasn't just the pub any more – it was also my home, the place where I lived. I was there on my own in the private bar, feverishly polishing tables and windowsills and chair-backs in preparation for an impending visit. I desperately wanted to avoid being there when this mysterious visitor arrived, because, although I had no idea what his name was, I could picture his face in my mind, and I knew that he was the embodiment of evil. However, I also knew with absolute certainty, as one does in dreams, that if I were to leave before thoroughly cleaning every corner of my house, something dark and terrible would happen to me anyway.

In the manner of nightmares, I repeatedly reached a point where I thought I had finished my task, only to notice with a sudden thrill of horror that a corner or a table-top or a shelf had been missed in my frantic attempt to get the work done. At last, just as I heard the sound of car tyres crunching on the gravel outside, I reckoned that the whole place was done. Almost sobbing with urgency I rushed to the back door and had actually gripped the handle and was about to turn it and leave, when my heart seemed to stop. I'd missed something. Right in the middle of the room, between me and the front door, stood a small table, smeared, stained – obviously not cleaned. How could I have missed it? As the handle of the front door turned and the door itself began slowly to open, I rushed forward, frantically wiped the surface of the table with the cloth that was still in my hand, and threw myself in the direction of the back door, passing through and slamming it behind me just as a shadowy figure appeared at the other end of the bar.

The next part of the dream was like one of those adventure films where somebody tries to shake off a 'tail'. I found myself climbing in and out of taxis, ducking into department stores and leaving through side doors, even lying on top of a moving train at one point, and finally rowing a small boat across a vast, silent lake towards a tiny island sitting in a low cloud of mist. Abruptly, I was on the island, and, rather improbably I suppose, walking towards a little tree-surrounded pub whose twinkling lights and general homeliness seemed to offer safety and comfort. Inside, sitting at a table in the furthest corner, I found, to my great joy, Greg smiling and beckoning just as he'd always done in the past before he got religious.

I moved towards him, filled with relief and pleasure, but even as I neared the table and was about to sit down, a dreadful foreboding swept over me. It was too late – I was already seated. Looking up, I watched Greg's face change before my eyes, the friendly smile twisting itself into one of vicious triumph. A silent scream filled my head as I realized that I had not avoided my visitor after all.

I really believed that I woke from this nightmare with an audible scream, but when Violet came into the room a few seconds later she didn't look as if she'd heard anything like that.

'You haven't touched your tea,' she said, and then suspiciously, 'you haven't been back to sleep, have you?'

I held my hand out in her direction.

'Violet – please, could you just hold on to me for a moment? I had the most awful nightmare a moment ago. I...I can't quite believe it wasn't real just at the minute.'

Despite the tremors that were still rocking my consciousness, it was lovely to see the look of compassion in my wife's eyes as she sat on the edge of the bed and took my hand.

'What sort of nightmare?'

'Oh, about someone coming to get me, and Greg in a sort of pub, and – oh, I don't want to think about it.' I grabbed a passing impulse and hung on to it before it could escape. 'Violet, I do love you very much, you know.'

Violet's eyes brightened a little for a moment, then she sighed and shook her head very slightly. It was only about the third time I'd said it since we got married.

'Do you?' she said, in a small, not very hopeful voice. 'Do you really love me?'

'I'm going to get up now,' I told her, 'and I'm going to go down to the river for a walk, and when I come back – I'll tell you what I've decided to do.'

We were both silent for a short time. Violet gently disengaged her hand and stood up slowly. 'I'll go and start the dinner,' she said, 'and I'll see you later.'

I didn't walk to the river in the end. It occurred to me as I went out of the door that there would probably be quite a lot of people down there, and just at the moment I wasn't interested in seeing anybody else. The tiniest little glimmer of hope was shining somewhere on the edge of my inner vision and I wanted a chance to look at it properly – to see if it would lead me anywhere. I had told Violet that I loved her. I had actually told Violet that I loved her!

I had seen, if only momentarily, her eyes fill with something that wasn't exasperation, and she had held my hand and almost been – she'd almost been something that she used to be a lot. She had almost been a little bit happy.

I drove up to the top of Vokes Hill, left the car on the rough old parking space by the road, and walked slowly out towards the edge of the valley, humming very quietly to myself. There was a little spur of soft turf just where the level began to drop. It was one of my favourite places – always had been. I sat there and stared across the valley, hoping that some inspiration would hit me or fill me or do something to me.

What actually happened was that I suddenly began to cry again. I couldn't help it. This time it poured out like one of those geysers that spout hot water. I was so glad there was nobody else about because this wasn't a gentle, beautiful little weep, it was a release – I assumed – of years of holding everything in and back inside the part of me that felt things and didn't know how to express them. A small detached part of myself listened with amazement to the whooping, sobbing, desperate noises that I was making, noises that I'd never made before as far as I could remember.

Then the crying died down a bit, but only a bit, and I started to speak to someone. I hadn't a clue who I thought was listening, but I certainly seemed to want to communicate with him or her.

'The thing is,' I said, in between sobs and whoops, 'that I can't stand Dan being all grown-up and not liking me so much and looking at me as if he thinks I'm an idiot. Y'see, he always really looked up to me and he really – you know – really wanted to please me because I was his dad and we always did everything together and now we don't. And what's going to happen if little Curly suddenly gets all stroppy when she's a big girl – I can't, I just can't! And I want Violet to be happy, but I'm no good at saying the things that she...the things that she wants me to say, although I did just now and I wish, I really wish that I could be what she wants, but I'm just not…'

My emotions gradually came under control as I released all these swirling thoughts. Finally, I was just producing little sniffing noises, with an occasional shudder. I wiped my nose with a fragment of tissue excavated from an inside pocket and buried the result under a little tombstone of turf. Then I picked a tall grass stalk with a brown bobbly bit on top, and began to address it in quiet, serious tones.

'Now,' I said, 'we come to the subject of Greg. You' – I jabbed my finger accusingly at the grass stalk – 'have somehow managed to ensnare him into your *thing*, whatever your thing is, just when I am most in need of the kind of exclusive attention that, in the past, I've tended to find a trifle annoying. You bring this Steve person along with Greg to *my* pub for reasons best known to yourself, and force me to listen to him being tactful and generous and – uugh!' I made being-sick noises. The grass stalk waved gently and serenely. It seemed to have no shame.

The next five minutes takes some explaining, or rather, it would do, if it could be explained. It was as though some other fairly long chunk of dialogue had been going on underneath all the crying and my haranguing of the local vegetation. Suddenly I wasn't talking to that grass stalk any more, in fact I threw it to one side and looked out over the valley as I spoke.

'What's going to happen if I give in and go with you? What am I going to have to say and do? Who am I going to have to tell? Which branch of the living dead will I be publicly identifying with? What will Violet say? What will Greg say next week when he suddenly announces that he's made a mistake and he wants to be a Jehovah's Witness instead, and I'm all committed to the thing that he's just left? Will we still go down the pub?' Pause. 'What *will* Violet say?'

As I asked that last question for the second time, I saw Violet's face again, full of hope as it had fleetingly appeared that morning, and I knew – don't ask me how, but I did – that her tears and her hope and a lot of the sadness she'd been feeling were – well – inhabited by the person I was talking to up on top of this hill. I know that sounds absurd, but there was a solid reality in this new piece of knowledge that was simply unavoidable. I shook my head, embarrassed suddenly by the proximity of my own thoughts. What was going on? Was I talking to God? Was he talking to me?

I became aware, as I sat there, that there was something different about me – about the way I felt to myself, I mean. For some minutes I simply couldn't pin it down, but then it dawned on me what it was. Just for a few minutes I had actually felt more or less at peace.

Peace?

I'd almost forgotten what peace meant. I'd got used to living with a constant layer of tension. In bed at night I often had to relax the muscles of my neck by an effort of will before I was able to truly rest my head and get to sleep. For a little while the springs inside me had been released and allowed to move back into the shape they were intended to be. It was a strange, almost tipsy feeling. Very pleasant – very pleasant indeed.

I drove back down the hill in a dream, humming to myself as I had done earlier. I had no idea what I was going to say to Violet, and there was no plan of action in my mind at all. It didn't seem to matter somehow. I wondered if everything would revert to normal as soon as I got back home.

'Don't let it,' I implored the grass stalk substitute as I pulled into the front drive and stopped the car.

Violet and I were oddly shy of each other in the period leading up to lunch. It was rather nice in a way – a bit like we used to be when we were courting. Both children were out for the day, thank goodness. Neither of us wanted to spoil the moment by bringing up the thorny subject of 'what I was going to do'. Violet did in the end, though. I knew she would. Despite this little lull she was desperate for something to change, and I still felt a fear deep inside me at the thought that she might stop loving me and move away into herself forever.

'What have you decided to do?'

That's what she said just as I picked up my glass of traditional lemonade, and I still had no answer prepared for her. What *was* I going to do? Silently I asked myself the question again. What am I going to do? What am I...?

'I'd like to invite Greg and his friend Steve round to eat with us one night soon.'

She looked steadily at me for a moment, then spoke quietly but with a firm challenge in her voice. 'What about the day after tomorrow?'

I swallowed. 'The day after tomorrow would be fine.'

'All right, then.'

'I love you, Violet.'

Four times in one lifetime! I could hardly believe it. Nor could she.

'I love you too, but, Paul, if something doesn't change...'

I reached across. 'Have a tissue. Leave the washing up and come for a walk up on the hill with me. Indulge my lunacy. There's a grass stalk I want you to meet.'

Speaking Up

By Joe Plass

Lawrence sat on the pavilion steps smiling mechanically. He had received an unexpected phone call from a former workmate at the beginning of the week, asking if he could possibly do an old friend a favour and stand in for the East Hinchley third team as they were short of players. It had seemed a lovely idea at the time. He didn't know any other members of the team, but that didn't really matter. All week Lawrence had been picturing idyllic scenes featuring himself basking in the August sun, or exchanging lazy comments in the pavilion with friendly locals. He seemed to recall from occasional visits in the past that East Hinchley Common had three or four gigantic horse-chestnut trees spaced across it, and it was under one of these that Lawrence had looked forward to whiling away a couple of hours or so while his team was batting, immersed in the pleasures of idleness. He had particularly relished the prospect of placing a Scotch egg and a large plastic bottle containing diluted blackcurrant by his side. Slowly and carefully he would lean back against the tree, fondly selecting a Sherlock Holmes story from his well-thumbed *Complete Works* edition.

Now Saturday afternoon had come and this Utopia was fading as the dreaded 'I don't know anybody' feeling began to set in and the old friend was nowhere in sight. Worse, half an hour ago, before more than a couple of others had arrived at the ground, his loathed clumsiness had reared its ugly head once more, resulting in the breakage of what Lawrence suspected was a sentimentally sacred vase which had been standing, shining and majestic, on a thin, wooden shelf in the pavilion. It had been the faintest of brushes but more than enough to jolt the bloody thing on to the hard floor and into a thousand pieces. Lawrence, like a true English gentleman, had surveyed the immediate area for witnesses and, finding that he was alone in the building, had left the scene of the crime as quickly and quietly as possible, to go for a little walk. Now he was back.

He shifted his position on the steps, lit a cigarette and waited for his friend to come.

Lawrence was sixty years old. He had a short, unruly crop of grey hair, a round, gentle face, and a lazy disposition which he had carried with him, contentedly or otherwise, for the whole of his life. He lived in a small, badly maintained cottage a few miles from Hinchley. His great loves were tatty detective books which he'd forgotten the ends of, ludicrously sugary tea and cigarettes. Most of his time was spent in the company of at least one of these things.

As a very young child he had actually been a thinker, someone whose thoughts rarely engaged with the present, an unusual state of mind which, coupled with a fiercely analytical intelligence, made living life at the speed of others tiresome to say the least. He might have become something special if anyone had encouraged him, but nobody understood or talked about 'gifted children' in those days, least of all his own mother. Lawrence was clumsy – scatty minded. That's what his mother had decided he was, and he had never dared to disagree with her – not about that nor indeed anything else. In fact, he had got out of the habit of being right. He had got into the habit of assuming that he would be wrong.

When he looked back to the part of his life when he was little, so many incidents sprang to mind – visions of himself protesting his point so furiously that tears of passion would form, and his mother, a calm, rational woman with a deceptively sharp, merciless tongue cutting him short without explanation, but always with the simple patronizing words, 'You're wrong, Lawrence.' Always stated in a controlled, singsong voice, and always accompanied by the same gentle, pitying shake of the head.

Lawrence stretched. Quite a lot of people had arrived by now, and still he had failed to make contact with anybody. He stood up and strolled back into the pavilion.

The kitchen seemed to be swamped with loud, middle-aged ladies, each struggling to create her own area of space to put the finishing touches to a dish that would be unveiled at tea. Everyone was *ever so* polite, the air rife with pleases, thankyous and excuse mes, but the women prepared their own dishes with every bit as much competitiveness as their male partners played cricket. It was not entirely unheard of for a ham and leek quiche to be sabotaged wilfully when its creator's back was turned.

Through the pavilion window, Lawrence could see small boys playing a ferociously fast and important game using the side of the pavilion as their wicket, and bronzed old men in Marks and Spencer shirts sitting languidly on benches around the park, presumably discussing batting technique and cricket etiquette as they smoked their long wooden pipes.

There were men, other players in the forthcoming match, he supposed, busy in conversation at the bar, perhaps catching up on each other's safe, uneventful lives. Lawrence joined them reluctantly, the thought of that infernal vase still playing on his mind. Someone had obviously cleared it up. Glancing along the bar at the other players he was comforted by the fact that he was not alone in age or fitness. A large, balding, pig-like man, wearing virtually skintight whites and a dirty mauve headband turned to Lawrence and mumbled in a thick Lancashire accent something that sounded like 'Old Bogsy ain't got no balls.'

Lawrence chuckled softly, making a vain attempt to look and sound as if he had found the comment incredibly amusing, but at the same time strangely perceptive. But the pig just glowered at him through pursed lips and growled something to his friend, then left with one last piercing stare, perhaps in search of some food.

This shook Lawrence. For a time he could not make out the reasoning behind the man's hostility. However, after chewing on the problem he came to the conclusion that the pig's comment had been absolutely literal, and that Bogsy (another fat, unintelligible local, he guessed) had in fact not got any cricket balls, a fair comment before a cricket match, by anyone's standards. A chuckle was not the right response. Lawrence sank further down on his seat and cursed himself for being such a cretin. Sighing heavily, he ordered a packet of roasted peanuts, paid for them, then rose from his stool and trudged despondently outside for a much needed cigarette.

Still the friend had not arrived. It was gradually dawning on him that, with the exception of himself, there was not a person here who knew about his inclusion in the team. Lawrence grimaced worriedly. After smoking for a while, he trod on his cigarette butt then went back into the pavilion and took the plunge into the changing room. Finding a hook and a seat, he pushed his embarrassingly tatty kitbag under the bench.

The room was full, the air claustrophobic with nauseous smells of sweaty boxes and ancient pullovers which had seen one summer too many. The atmosphere was coarse with shouts and dirty laughs. A mixture of ferocious late cuts and glorious off drives swept the air of the changing room as players rehearsed for the coming battle.

The players greeted Lawrence with neither animosity nor interest, and gradually the shackles of recent events began to fall away. He found himself quite relishing the prospect of a gloriously sunny Saturday afternoon spent on newly-cut grass. After a while he began to receive some puzzled frowns from team mates but this didn't perturb him especially. Surely his friend must arrive soon.

Lawrence was hoping for a comfortable batting position, number seven would do nicely, he thought, not so high up that he would be of too much importance, but essential enough to be unable to umpire. In a match of this kind a member of the batting team would almost invariably be asked to undertake that thankless task.

Yes, he was quite looking forward to it. Lawrence was not a particularly good batsman, he had never been able to bowl legally and his rheumatism put paid to any full length dives in the covers when fielding, but none of these things really mattered. It was the luscious combination of new and old smells which he loved, the seam on an unused ball, the militant pride taken in dilapidated willow. Most of all he loved it when he wasn't actually playing, slouched on a deck chair in the sun outside the pavilion, with a predictable paperback and the inevitable cigarette. A pity, though, that the fondly remembered chestnut trees appeared to have been chopped down.

Lawrence undressed thoughtfully and opened his bag. His trousers weren't too bad, a little short in the leg perhaps, but passable for the third eleven. His jumper was a different matter altogether. There was no getting away from the fact that it definitely had a faint pink tinge to it and, curiously, one sleeve seemed to be somehow longer than the other. Batting pads were no better. Beautifully made they may have been, but now they were reduced to pitiful slabs of grey. Lawrence hastily pushed them to the bottom of his bag.

Suddenly the door was pushed open and the crescendo of tasteless jokes and dirty jibes lulled. A small, stocky man in perfect whites, with a pair of ultra-violet sunglasses tucked into his shirt pocket, marched into the room. He stood in the centre of the changing room playing the captain's role to the extreme, tense and erect like a general surveying his troops. Looking around the team he produced the most hideously fake smile Lawrence had ever seen, then, pausing for a second and taking a deep breath, he summoned all the volume and intensity he could muster and bawled at the top of his voice, with fist clenched:

'Ha-a-a-ave it!!!'

The rest of the team leapt to their feet, and with the same extraordinary enthusiasm responded by repeating this cry, twisting their faces into ghoulish expressions to put as much into those two words as possible. Lawrence, who was totally unprepared for this outburst, was only able to respond with a John Major-like twitter which was far from being in unison with the rest of the players.

After they'd finished changing, the team sat rather sheepishly, waiting expectantly for their captain, who was making an elaborate show of oiling a dashingly handsome cricket bat. This task fulfilled, and his navy-blue cap placed symmetrically on his shiny scalp, he turned to the team, eyebrows raised arrogantly, and with a flurry of theatrical gestures proceeded to regurgitate several portions of his vast knowledge of the game. Nobody was about to interrupt him.

Some minutes into this enthralling lecture he stopped in full flow, his eyes, like those of an angry hawk, boring into Lawrence's startled face. There followed a horrible silence, in which neither man seemed able to summon appropriate words. The captain's hand gradually rose and then shot out like a dart, the long index finger quivering with emotion.

'You! Who *are* you?' he hissed menacingly through clenched teeth.

Lawrence was so taken aback by this outburst that the matey laugh with which he had meant to reassure and disarm the man who stood before him actually came out as a smutty little snigger, a response which had little effect other than slightly to change the captain's complexion, at best a deep red, but now an unhealthy purple. This facial firework display did nothing to comfort Lawrence, who was by now close to weeping. Could it be that someone knew about the vase? He cleared his throat and offered what, at this stage, felt like a hopelessly feeble explanation, even though it was the plain truth.

'Bryan told me Hinchley were a bit short so I decided to come along.'

Even before the sentence was completed Lawrence knew that the tone was all wrong. It just hadn't sounded right. Once more he accompanied his words with something that came out as a deranged cackle, forcing the other man to take a sharp step backwards. Recovering his composure, the captain drew himself to his full height and spoke in the same seething tones.

'So-o-o-o?' he screeched, dangerous restraint stretched across his face.

Lawrence caught his breath. Why was this fiendish little man so intent on humiliating him in front of all these people, and what was the bloke's problem anyway? He rarely lost his temper, well, he rarely had cause to, and wouldn't normally have the courage, but it had been a horrible day so far, and the fragile strings of his patience and sanity were stretched to breaking point. Let's face it, there was no possible chance in hell that he was wrong on this occasion. He'd been asked to come, and he'd come. Surely it was time for him to speak up for himself, to show this sneering big-mouth that he wasn't the imbecile he seemed to think he was, to bring the power-crazed bully down a peg or two. Yes, this time, he was right! He sprang up from the bench and bearing down on the equally furious captain, began to shout:

'I am very, very sorry if being part of the same team as me causes you to burst a blood vessel, but there is no reason whatsoever why you should treat me like some kind of...'

Lawrence stopped suddenly as he took a second look at the kitbag by the captain's foot. In very large green capital letters, he read the following words:

LITTLE COMMON C.C. 1st XI

Lawrence blinked and picked up his bag. In one final, superficial attempt to retain his dignity, he nodded curtly to the captain before walking quickly through the door, out of the pavilion, and down to the main road. He didn't look back once as he trudged despondently towards the bus stop.

Small World

They say you should never go back.

I read a short story once that began with those exact words, and broadly speaking I suppose at the time when I read them I would have agreed. You never know what's going to happen when you take the risk of going back. That's why I was so surprised to find myself on Platform Nine of Clapham Junction Railway Station at a quarter to ten one cold autumn morning, probably the coldest of the year so far, waiting for a train that would take me to Winchester for the first time for more than two decades.

With less than ten minutes to go before the train was due to arrive, part of me didn't really believe I would actually get on when it rumbled to a halt. Why in a month of Sundays, I kept asking myself, should I actively court the pain and disappointment that could easily result from such an emotionally loaded expedition? What was the point of risking some kind of inner disaster when, at a pinch, I could manage to go on living with the tightly tied knot that had been in my stomach since I was a young boy? It was my wife who had finally persuaded me to do the thing I feared so much.

'You may be able to go on living with it,' she said one day, 'but I'm not sure the rest of us can. Seriously, John, why don't you pick a day and just go. I know it won't be easy, but you'll be so glad when you've done it. I'll come with you if you want. I tell you what – I'll take you out and buy you an Indian as a reward when you get back.'

She was deliberately being flippant about something that really mattered to her, but she was right. There's something about the idea of an Indian meal that brightens just about anything up. It was the trigger. I said I'd go, but on my own.

'Winchester, Winchester, Winchester...' I whispered the word neurotically over and over to myself as I paced up and down the long platform trying to keep warm. For me, the very word sagged with significance, like one of those poems that tries to make you feel too much.

I did board the 9.56 when it arrived. If I hadn't been as frozen as I was I might have dithered and changed my mind, but it was *so* wonderful to step into the heated interior of the train. Not only that, but I also found a vacant window seat by a table almost immediately.

On the other side of the table sat a young chap of about eighteen, lost in the private world of his personal stereo. Outside this little universe all that could be heard of the recorded sound was a featureless buzz. Settling back into the warmth and comfort of my new surroundings I found myself idly wondering if this was a happy person. He looked quite together and content I thought, the sort of young man who is just beginning to feel a genuine confidence in himself. He had a well-cared-for, secure look about him. Good parents probably. A mother who'd consistently done her very best for him, a father who was never intrusive but always there if he was needed when things started to fall apart. Sports. Advice. All that stuff. Yes, by the look of him that was exactly the sort of father he'd got. And would he realize just how bloody fortunate he was in that respect? Oh, no! You could bet your life he...

I squirmed in my seat as all the old boringly familiar feelings of helpless rage began to mount in me. How long was I going to have to put up with the past reaching out to grab me by the throat like this? What a maniac I was becoming. Pushing the hair brusquely back from my forehead with one hand, I dragged my attention away from the innocent music lover on the other side of the table, and gazed out of the window. As if in some fever dream, I rehearsed the past in my mind as I had done a thousand times, helplessly aware that ten thousand repetitions would never make any difference to the way things had been.

I never had fully understood why my parents separated. I lived with my mother, a very efficient, undemonstrative, quietly unhappy woman. The only thing she ever said about the failure of her marriage was in answer to an unusually direct question when I was about ten.

'Why did Daddy go away and leave us when I was little?'

'Your father can only cope with very small worlds.'

That was all she said and all she would say. It was typically enigmatic. What was a ten-year-old supposed to do with that? I hadn't the faintest idea what she was talking about. Perhaps if I'd thought about it a little more I might have begun to understand. After all, Dad had created a little world for him and me to be together in, and it hardly changed at all in the short time that I knew him.

It began a few days after my eighth birthday. Mother announced quite dispassionately one morning that my father had come back to England to live. He wanted to see me that afternoon in Winchester. Did I want to go?

I knew I had a dad, but he'd left when I was little more than a baby, so I had no memory of him at all. My mother kept no photographs of her ex-husband in our house. Many times, in the course of my early years, I had lain awake at night, picturing his face just above the end of the bed in the darkness of my room, and imagined making a special trip to find him. In my fantasies he was always overjoyed to see me. We would embrace, and he would explain why it had been so difficult for us to be together, and say how much he had missed me since going away.

Here was a chance to see him in reality. I felt shy but excited. I remember looking into my mother's face, searching for a clue to the solution of the obvious problem. Did she want me to go? But my mother's face never gave information of that sort. There were no clues.

'Yes, please,' I said, 'I'd like to go, mother.'

Later that morning my mother drove me to Winchester in our blue mini. We stopped just outside the 'Old Market Inn'. There was a man leaning against a gatepost a few yards away. Mother didn't even get out. So much for my secretly cherished dreams of parental reunion!

'That's your father,' she said, pointing. 'You'll like him. I'll pick you up again at five o'clock.'

Suddenly, there I was, at eight years of age, standing outside a pub in a strange city with a strange man, watching the familiar shape of our little car accelerate away and disappear round the corner. Looking back, I can hardly believe what my mother did. I cannot begin to imagine doing anything so clearly irresponsible with one of my own children. For a few seconds I did experience real panic, but small children readily accept bizarre things, and, in any case, my mother had told me I would like my father, and she was the sort of woman for whom every opinion laid down was a winning card. I had never known her to be wrong before.

Nor was she wrong now. All he said in a quiet, resonant voice as I walked hesitantly in his direction, was, 'John? I'm your dad,' but his eyes smiled from far inside and there was a feeling of safeness about him. I recall being obscurely pleased that he continued to lean on the gatepost as I moved towards him. He let me do the last bit of the trip.

This first meeting was a long way from the emotional splurge of my night-time fantasies, but from the moment I encountered my father's chuckling good humour I absolutely adored him. That day we sat on the grass outside the cathedral in the sunshine, and ate our way through a picnic he'd brought. I remember every crumb. There were three different kinds of sandwich – ham, banana and cheese – two kinds of cake – Battenburg and cherry – two chocolate biscuits wrapped in shiny coloured paper, and an apple each. There was a bottle filled with ready-diluted lemon squash and two disposable paper cups to drink it from.

He asked me questions about myself as we ate, listening in a very still way with his head on one side as I gained confidence and chattered away about home and school and friends and football.

When he asked me which team I supported I suspended the whole of my beloved Arsenal team and said, 'Which one do you support?'

'Aston Villa,' he replied.

'So do I,' I said, and from that day forward I did.

When we'd finished eating he packed everything away in a brown and green leather shopping bag and stood up.

'Well, John,' he smiled, 'do you think we're going to be pals?'

I looked at him then and thought to myself that he was a 'hands in his pockets' sort of man. His clothes were brown and soft, so were his face and hair. He was comfortably untidy and his eyes seemed a little bit hurt as well as being smiley and kind.

'Oh, yes, Dad,' I said, relishing this word that had suddenly become so unexpectedly and wonderfully substantial, 'we'll be pals all right.'

We spent the rest of the afternoon walking slowly round the inside of the cathedral, stopping every now and then for me to ask a question, or when Dad wanted to explain something. He seemed to know an awful lot about everything without having to use a guide, and I think I sensed, even then, that he was introducing me to something he loved.

Mother picked me up at five o'clock – on the dot, of course. She didn't get out of the car this time either, or even look in the direction of my father, as far as I could see. Poor Mother. I'm sure I must have rabbited on about my new 'pal' all the way back home, but all I can remember her saying was, 'I told you you'd like him.'

'But,' I said in real puzzlement to myself in bed that night, 'how could you possibly *not* like someone so nice?'

Three or four times a year for the next four years the pattern of that first visit was repeated. There might be fruit cake instead of Battenburg, and the weather might drive us under cover to eat our picnic sometimes, but in every other way our outings stayed exactly the same, from the brown and green leather shopping bag to the paper cups. It never struck me as odd that we always met in the same way, and always did the same things. On the contrary, I loved it. I loved him. It was simply the way things were. I didn't mind in the least that I never saw where he lived, and never really learned anything about the rest of his life, because we seemed to belong to each other totally for as long as those all too infrequent afternoons lasted, and that was all that mattered to me. As time went by Winchester Cathedral and everything connected with it glowed richly in my imagination with a sparkling Christmassy brightness, a reflection of the joy I found in just being there with my father.

He died at the wrong time, you see. I was twelve. It was two days before my next visit was due. When my mother gave me the news, delivered in that same dry, disinterested way, it was like being punched in the stomach very hard when you're not expecting it. And then – well, I've never been quite sure what happened then. I think I managed to switch something off right inside me, and I felt nothing. I don't know if I was ever quite able to forgive my mother for the way she dealt with me over my father's death. I wasn't taken to any kind of service and there was no grave because his body had been cremated. The ashes were distributed somewhere or other by somebody, my mother said, with an almost non-existent emphasis on the 'somebody', and that was it. He was gone. Nothing to remind me of him, and a complete inability to grieve. I don't think I shed a single tear.

The years went by. I grew up. I got married. My mother died. I had two children. I was very nearly happy – happy but for the nagging, ever-present knowledge that one day

I was going to have to deal with the little unexploded bomb that lay like a lump of cold metal in the pit of my stomach. I was never quite brave enough to face it, the mixture of grief, sorrow, heartache that might explode and tear me to pieces. I kept well away from Winchester.

Now my wife had talked me into going back. She had seen, over the years, how the pain of this emotional containment affected not just me but her and the children as well. Often it manifested itself in black moods that had no very clear link to the past, but were nevertheless closely connected with those distant days.

Sometimes, specific incidents triggered irrational bouts of anger. When Sam, aged nine, asked me why I supported a 'rubbish team' like Aston Villa, I flew into a terrible rage, demanding to know why I shouldn't and what it had got to do with him. For that brief, black period I felt as if I was eight years old and he was bullying me. Realizing what was really going on was so strange – like regaining consciousness after a particularly vivid dream. Poor, confused Sam forgave me freely.

Another time, I was walking around the local shopping precinct with my wife, when I happened to notice that a woman walking beside me was carrying a shopping bag that closely resembled the one my father used to pack our picnics in. Brown leather with inlaid green patches. The sight of it made me feel sick in my stomach. I was low for days. So many things…

Well, I was going to tackle it now. Soon after alighting from this train I would be stepping back into the only world that my father and I had ever shared. Resting my face against the cold surface of the window I closed my eyes and dozed fitfully for the rest of the hour-long journey.

By 11.15 I was sitting in the warmth and comfort of the 'Old Market Inn' in Winchester. The walk down from the station had set up such a screaming tension in me that my hands and teeth were tightly clenched by the time I turned into Market Street, but I was beginning to feel a little better now. I couldn't have faced going into the cathedral straight away, and the only delaying tactic that I could think of was the pub. I'm not a great drinker at the best of times, let alone on an occasion like this, so I simply ordered a hot chocolate and took it over to a seat by the window that looked out towards the cathedral. Resting my elbows on the table in front of me I cuddled the hot china mug in my hands. It felt like a mini-version of one of those old stone hotwater bottles that I could just remember having in bed with me when I stayed with my grandmother as a small child.

Through the window I could see, a hundred yards away, the west door of the cathedral, the door that my dad and I had walked through so many times. Now, on this desolately bleak October afternoon, a mere trickle of warmly dressed visitors was passing in and out of the building.

I decided to give myself a talking to.

'Now look!' I whispered into the side of my mug, 'you are an adult. You are not a child. You are allowed to choose what to do for yourself. If you decide to get up and walk back to the station and take the next train home, then that is fine. That is absolutely fine. You've lived with this fear in your gut for twenty years. You might as well put up with it for another decade or two. Why tear yourself to pieces for nothing? Give up! Go home! You don't even really know what you're looking for, and you probably won't find it here anyway. Apart from anything else, how are you going to handle a thumping great anticlimax, if that's what it turns out to be? Go on – go home. Finish your hot drink and get back to the station.'

Haranguing myself like this has always helped me to make decisions, and it did now. I stood up, buttoned my overcoat, wrapped my scarf round my neck, and left the pub. Seconds later, breathless with quivering anticipation and the icy cold, I was striding across the Close with almost robotic determination towards the west door. I was about to pay my first visit to Winchester Cathedral since the year of my twelfth birthday. As I reached the door and pushed it open I realized that it was also the only time I had ever entered it on my own.

Despite the cold I was perspiring heavily as I came through the inner door and stood motionless for a moment at the west end of the nave. The abruptly overpowering familiarity of my surroundings made me feel quite faint. Then, suddenly filled with a brittle excitement, I swung round and peered up at the strange jumble of stained-glass fragments that almost filled the top half of the west wall.

'What's that all about then, John?'

I remembered the question. I remembered my answer.

'Cromwell smashed a window, Dad, and the people saved the pieces and hid 'em and tried to put them back together later, but they couldn't get it right so they put them all over the place like a giant jigsaw puzzle so they'd still got their window, whatever old Cromwell thought he'd done. Is that right, Dad?'

It was right. It was right! Dad had told me, so it must be right.

I turned round and started to walk along the south aisle. I was in a trance. I was twelve years old. I remembered everything. There was Doctor Warton's memorial, and there, listening forever to their famous headmaster, were three of his pupils dressed in their funny old-fashioned clothes.

'Where will we find three little tiny monks, John?'

I was *so* proud.

'Over here, Dad, sitting by the bishop's feet.'

And then, a bit further up, the list of people from something called the Hampshire regiment, who had all been killed in the war.

'Listen, Dad! Listen! Listen! Listen to the names – Shadwell, Smallpiece, Smith, Spanner, Stammer, Steele, Stone. Are they real names, Dad?'

'Yes, they're real names and they really did die, son.'

On to the South Transept, and the oldest oak chairs in England.

'Are we allowed to sit on them, Dad?'

'Yes, go on. Nothing to say you can't, is there? They've put up with four hundred years of assorted English bottoms. If yours makes much difference it's probably time for them to be turned into firewood anyway.'

I always sat on both of them, enthralled by the thought of those hundreds and hundreds of different backsides perching there over the years.

Next came the grave of Isaak Walton, the fisherman, followed by the memorial to Bishop Wilberforce, son of the man who tried to free all the slaves. Over there were the Pilgrim Gates, and up to the left, in their chests on top of the wall, were the bones of the old kings. Most frightening to me as a small boy was the horrible cadaver of Bishop Fox in its tiny prison behind iron bars, put there by him to remind the world that no one lives forever.

Oh, Dad...

I came to a place where candles glowed and flickered on a wrought-iron stand. Taking a fresh candle I lit it from one of the others and put a coin in the nearby box. Stepping back, I stared at the little flame as it wavered and nearly died before starting to burn steadily. The candle was for my father. Its flame was alive, and he was dead. I began to perspire again. That bomb inside me was about to go off and I was terrified. Instinctively I moved away from a small group of people who were peering at something beside me, and turned quickly into the retrochoir, deserted now, but filled, like every other corner of this building, with four years of Dad and me.

'See those words under that grille, son? They're all about St Swithun, the saint of the cathedral. Do you remember what that first bit means?'

'Whatever partakes of God is safe in God. Right, Dad?'

'Right, son.'

I couldn't stand it any more. I had to get out. I set off down the north presbytery aisle, intending to head straight for the exit at the other end of the building, but a loud group of tourists forced me aside into the choir, and suddenly I knew, like a child desperate not to throw up in the wrong place, that I wasn't going to make it. I crumpled on to one of the front choir stalls at the foot of the presbytery steps, trying to look as if I was intensely interested in the tomb of Rufus, the Norman king who died mysteriously in the New Forest.

'What did they find when they opened old Rufus up, John?'

'An arrowhead, Dad. Somebody shot him!'

'Oh, Dad, oh, Dad! Why did you die?'

I slumped forward, my face in my hands and wept. The explosion wasn't as wildly violent as I'd feared, but the sobs that passed through my body in wave after shuddering wave shook everything in me. And there was so much anger in it. Grief I'd expected, but not anger. Perhaps that was why I'd switched off after that first thudding shock all those years ago. Probably I just couldn't handle the idea of expressing intense fury to someone I had loved so much.

I certainly expressed it now.

'You left me! You left me alone! You just left me! Oh, Dad, why did you leave me?'

Sheer strength of feeling drove me to my feet. As far as I can remember there was nobody else in the choir, but I honestly don't think I'd have noticed if there had been. And it was at that moment, through the tears that had waited so long to be shed, that I found my eyes fixed on Dad's favourite thing of all, the carved figure of Christ on the cross right at the centre of the great screen above the high altar.

For one of the very few times in my life, some words of Jesus came, quite unbidden, to my mind.

'My God! My God! Why have you forsaken me?'

Whatever partakes of God is safe in God.
'Is that right, Dad?'
'That's right, son.'
A small world.

Also by Adrian Plass available from HarperCollins *Publishers*:

The Sacred Diary of Adrian Plass Christian Speaker Aged 45³/₄

Illustrated by Dan Donovan

Certainly a little older, perhaps just a tiny bit wiser, Adrian Plass was amazed when his account of 'serious spiritual experiences' in *The Sacred Diary of Adrian Plass Aged 37³/₄* became widely read and appreciated as a funny book! More books have followed and now he's in demand as a public speaker all over the place. As we follow him to a variety of venues the reason why Christian speakers need travelling mercies becomes abundantly clear!

Many of the characters we met in the first *Sacred Diary* are with us again – Leonard Thynn, the Flushpools, Gerald (grown up now, of course!), Adrian's wife Anne, voluptuous Gloria Marsh, Edwin (the wise church elder) and the ever-religious Richard and Doreen Cook – as well as one or two new characters; Stephanie Widgeon, for instance, who only seems to have only one thing to say...

One last question – what is a banner ripping seminar?

Stress Family Robinson

The Robinson family – mother, father, two teenage sons and a six-year-old daughter who is everyone's favourite – are a typical Christian family – or *are* they?

Does life behind the front door of the tall, thin Victorian semi-detached where they live match up to (or even resemble) the image they convey at their parish church?

The one person who knows the Robinsons almost better than they know themselves is dear Dip Reynolds – trusted friend-extraordinaire who has a few surprising secrets of her own to reveal…

The Sacred Diary Trilogy

The Sacred Diary of Adrian Plass Aged 37 3/4
The Horizontal Epistles of Andromeda Veal
The Theatrical Tapes of Leonard Thynn

Here to enjoy in one volume is Adrian Plass's much-loved comic trilogy. *The Sacred Diary of Adrian Plass Aged 37 3/4* records the trials and tribulations of Adrian, amiable but somewhat inept Christian husband and father, who decides to keep 'a sort of spiritual log for the benefit of others'. We are introduced to a glorious gallery of characters, including Adrian's patient wife Anne, their outrageous son Gerald, tippling Leonard Thynn, the gloomily devout Flushpools, and the 'small but powerful' Andromeda Veal.

In *The Horizontal Epistles of Andromeda Veal*, fiery young Andromeda is feeling lonely and vulnerable in hospital, apparently abandoned by her warring parents. Anne Plass mobilizes the whole church into letter-writing action, and Andromeda even finds herself writing a letter to God...

In *The Theatrical Tapes of Leonard Thynn*, well-meaning Leonard takes it upon himself to record the church's drama meetings. Doing a simple little sketch about Daniel in the lion's den should be straightforward...then again, maybe not.

The Growing Up Pains of Adrian Plass

Adrian Plass tells the story of his progress of faith with disarming honesty and the usual irresistible humour.

'Asked to leave' his grammar school, he eventually became a desperately lonely student at Bristol Old Vic Theatre School. Turned away even from the vicarage door, things only looked up when he met and married Bridget, a fellow student. Together they took up jobs in childcare.

Adrian's first brush with the media came when he heard that a television company was looking for 'six ordinary people' to take part in a new kind of late-night religious programme, 'Company'.

Although the rest is history, there were to be many more down times for Adrian, in the events of life and in his relationship with God. Departing from the usual formula of the 'Christian paperback' he tells it all.

Cabbages for the King

Cabbages for the King is a fabulous collection of jokes, stories, sketches and verse – most are humorous, a few are sad and serious, and the rest are beyond definition.

They are his 'cabbages' and Adrian the greengrocer – an ordinary man trying to live up to a high calling. Adrian, however, is quick to point out that whereas he will be known by his fruit when he gets to heaven, the greengrocer will be known by his fruit *and* veg.

An Alien at St Wilfred's

- Who wants to poison the organist?
- Why is the overhead projector so very annoyed?
- Who made the vicar burst into tears in his own pulpit?
- What on earth is happening to the church lighting?
- Why did four sane Anglicans meet on top of the tower in a raging storm?
- What is going on?

It's very simple – there is an alien at St Wilfred's!

This is the story of Nunc, the small alien, who comes to Earth and learns to speak in Prayer Book English – all told in the inimitable style of best-selling author Adrian Plass.